Trevor Knibb was born on 9th April 1944, at Kenton, Middlesex, and has two older brothers. Educated at The Boys Harrow High School, he left there to work on his elder brother's farm in Cornwall. After several years, he bought his own small holding and kept a large herd of pigs and beef.

Subsequently, moving to a totally different career, he launched a highly successful hair and beauty supply company. Slightly more recently, he developed a touring and camping park on some of the farmland from which he sold to retire.

Over the years, he has been a postman, salesman, hair salon owner and restaurateur. Now residing in Devon, he devotes his spare time to write fictional novels.

He has a wide range of interests which have included scuba diving, base jumping, world war two history, UFOs, wildlife and many more.

Trevor Knibb

The Gargoyle

Austin Macauley Publishers™
London • Cambridge • New York • Sharjah

A CIP catalogue record for this title is available from the British Library.

ISBN 9781398449718 (Paperback)
ISBN 9781398449725 (Hardback)
ISBN 9781398449732 (ePub e-book)

www.austinmacauley.com

First Published 2022
Austin Macauley Publishers Ltd®
1 Canada Square
Canary Wharf
London
E14 5AA

Characters

Terry Knight – Ex Special Forces
Lydia Knight – Terry's wife
Jason Knight – Son of Terry and Lydia
Natasha Knight – Daughter of Terry and Lydia
Sophia Webber – Estate Agent's assistant
Van Driver – Works for a local supermarket
John Desmond Hargreaves – Estate Agent
Lorry Driver – Works for a Sewage Company
Mrs 'Minnie' Winston – Café Owner
Harry Welford – Local Sheep Farmer
Harvey Trelease – Research Scientist
Doctor Jackson – Local GP
Kevin Brent – Research Scientist
Wendy Winston – Minnie Winston's Daughter
Ho Sing – Local Coroner and Solicitor
Doctor Faulkner – Director of Operations' at Porton Down Research Division
Davy 'Bomber' Bates – Ex Special Forces
Di – Davy's girlfriend
Kyle – Special Forces Operative
Wan – Foreign Thug
Jo – Foreign Thug
The Gargoyle – Himself

Prologue

The red-ringed eyes, which followed the man who was busy at a table, were filled with malice and hate. The chain which attached it to the side of the cage rattled as it shook the manacle fixed round its limb. It had constantly worried at the joint where it connected to the chain and over the years of its incarceration, the joint was now dangerously thin but as yet unnoticed by its captor.

The man, wearing a white coat, looked up at it and in a voice, that was used to being obeyed, told it to be quiet. The response was another malevolent look, thin lips drawn tight across a hairy jaw line which was split by a double line of uneven sharp fangs. The man gave a small grunt of satisfaction as he picked up a hypodermic syringe and inserted the needle into a small bottle of amber fluid. Drawing back the plunger, the syringe gently sucked in the liquid until it was full. He turned and walked towards the cage and without another word wound the handle of the small winch which tightened the chain attached to the creature inside, dragging it to the side. When this had been done, he went to the cage door, opened it and went inside. The eyes followed every movement, drool dripped from the malformed jaws and it shook itself in anticipation of the pain it knew was to come.

In its poor life, it had only known pain and suffering from its first memories inside this hated cage. 19 years in all but, of course, it had no means of knowing this. It seemed an eternity.

The syringe held in the man's hand came ever nearer. It writhed and squirmed, trying to get further away without success. A mewing sound emitted from it gaining volume and mucus dripping from its nostrils.

"Keep still," the man commanded, steadying his gloved hand as he lined up the needle with the limb trapped against the cage bars. He looked at it without sympathy. He had created this and he was proud of the success the experiment had proved. He was at the very brink of the rewards that this would bring. His masters would be delighted at the results of his work and he knew he could look forward to huge rewards, both financial and career wise, but this was not really what had driven him on to take the risks he had to achieve this breakthrough in science. It was enough to know it had been him that had done it.

The tip of the needle touched the skin. It jumped away from the contact and the man cursed.

"Keep still," he commanded again, this time with an edge to his voice.

God! This creature was huge, nearly six-and-a-half feet tall with muscles, which bulged from the sack like coat it wore and it was so ugly, slightly hunchbacked and very hairy, even he could not believe how the experiments had transformed this thing. That it was very intelligent was obvious to him and it appeared that its sensory organs were very highly developed. He had tested it, at least as much as he could. He knew that its hearing was extremely acute as was its sense of smell. The bulge above either side of its nostrils gave testament to the kind of scenting power that a dog might have. Probably in excess of 40 times that of a 'human'. He was not so sure about the eyes. They did not seem to see so clearly in daylight but he had proved that its sight in almost total darkness was remarkable.

He came nearer and as he did so, the creature gave a supreme wrench of its trapped limb, the shackle bolt weakened over the years with continuous rubbing, slowly bent apart until with a slight crack it parted the two side of the shackle falling with a loud clunk to the floor. For a brief second or two neither moved. Then the man, suddenly realising the danger, jumped back but too slowly. The creature was between him and the cage door which he had left open. He gradually extended his hand which still held the syringe.

"Get back, get back," he was pleading now. The long handled electric goad was outside the cage, propped against the table. The creature peered at him and snarled, spittle spraying out of its mouth over him. It looked at the open door and while its poor misshapen body was nothing like anyone had ever seen, there was no doubting the intelligence behind the eyes. It sensed freedom. They circled each other until the man sprang away towards the doorway. Again, far too slowly. The creature whirled round and with tremendous force slammed an arm against him, the hooked claws which protruded from the end, catching the man against the face, ripping the flesh off in strips, blood pulsing immediately from the wound. The syringe skittered across the floor as his hand opened, dropping it. He screamed in agony but still managed to evade the other arm which threatened to enclose him and turning, rushed through the cage door which he tried to swing shut. He almost succeeded but as he tried to ram the bolt home, the door was slammed against him and slowly forced back open. He released his grip and staggered backwards towards the table and the electric goad but didn't quite make it. Another violent blow sent him flying forwards and as he fell, his head smashed against the edge of the table and with a groan collapsed onto the floor. The creature stood over him, blood still dripping from the claws. It jerked violently in sudden pain and spun away shrieking. So intent had it been on its attack, it had not seen the other white coated man enter the room and pick up the goad which he now had slammed against its ribcage. The electric charge built up inside exploded with a sizzle.

In an instant, the second man grabbed his colleague's arm and with difficulty dragged him through to the next room while holding the goad in the other hand, pointing it at the creature which still writhed in pain. An ordinary person would have been left powerless with the shock. 50,000 volts, sometimes enough to kill a man but this…this…thing was still standing. It shook its huge deformed head and focused its eyes on the two men. Snuffling, it lumbered towards them stopping as the goad was raised again. Then lunged forward again, reeling back as the goad caught it, falling against the laboratory's tables, sending equipment cascading to the ground. Some cables became tangled in this causing more damage. Computers and screens smashed as they were dragged off the tables. Glass shards from the broken retorts glistened in the harsh lighting. In the seconds while it recovered, the man managed to drag his partner to the next door. Pulling him through the opening, he rammed his shoulder against the heavy door closing it just in time as the creature launched a furious attack on the other side. Claws grinding and scraping against the wood. Slivers of wood flicking off onto the floor. The man slid the two well-greased bolts into the holes and secured the door. Only then did he have time to inspect the injured man. Several flaps of skin hung down his face bleeding profusely. The top of his white coat was soaked with his blood and had now spattered onto his friend's. The main concern was with his head which had caught the edge of the table with such force. The second man gently placed his fingers against the neck, feeling for a pulse. Nothing! The head was badly damaged with matter beginning to seep out of the fractured skull. He was dead!

A loud but muffled, moaning cry split the air with sound from beyond the door.

* * * * *

Chapter One
Arrival 20 Years Later

Trelease House lay in a valley on a flat area of land between two low hills which ran north-west to the coast terminating in a dramatic, almost shear drop to the sea. A small river wandered to the south of the house, spreading out over the land in a multitude of rivulets to saturate the surface peaty soil, turning it into a glutinous, stinking marshland before gathering together once again to gain speed as it approached the rockier land, whereupon its nature changed from one of a slow body of water to a tumultuous one, gurgling, churning, sparkling as it did so as it roared down through a culvert, bouncing over the exposed rocks before entering a tunnel cut into the rock near an old abandoned mine engine house and add it before re-appearing again just below the steep edge of the cliff and then falling like a silver ribbon to the sea nearly 200 feet below. A small footbridge allowed access across the river near a large extensive woodland with a little footpath leading to the back of the house. In the other direction, the path meandered through the trees and then through the huge ugly piles of rock spoil dumped over a long period of time when the mine had been a working one until eventually reaching and joining the coastal path. Further along the coastal path near to the old mine workings, a much wider and larger bridge crossed the river by the tunnel where the river went underground, a track then went away towards the house and then joined the gravel drive. This roadway linked the house to the public road, coming to meet it in a wide sweep up the hill, which gave Terry Knight, his wife, Lydia, son, Jason and daughter, Natasha, a fantastic panoramic view of almost the whole valley giving way to the sea sparkling in the autumn sunlight in the distance.

They stared at the view, Terry having brought the Volvo XC90 to a stop at the entrance to the drive.

"What do you think then?" he said as they opened their doors and gathered around him, standing in a group. He put one of his arms around Lydia's waist and the other across the shoulders of his daughter. For a moment, nobody said a word. Then, everyone wanted to speak at once.

"Wow!" Natasha exclaimed.

"What a lovely position," Jason murmured.

Lydia tightened her entwined arm around Terry and looking up at him with her amazingly clear blue eyes, said, "You said it was special and it is. You know I had my doubts seeing as you did not have time to let me see it before you clinched the deal."

"I had to move fast as you know. Otherwise we might have lost it. I couldn't have believed just how cheap it was but only if I completed the deal quickly. It would appear they were very keen to move away. Been on the market for a while, I believe."

Terry was 50 years old, born just outside London, youngest son out of the three boys his parents reared. He was tall, 6' 1" with short dark brown hair just starting to go silver grey at the fringes, also with blue eyes, although his were startlingly piercing giving the appearance of looking through to your soul when he turned them upon you. His muscular frame with wide shoulders, straight back, a determined set to his jaw but with the many little lines engraved on his face, especially around his eyes, giving the impression of someone who could laugh easily but at the same time an attitude of authority and an air of slight sadness of things seen in his life but not talked about gave him a look of a man who had a service history in the armed services. He had, having been in the army for more than 25 five years, graduating to take part in special forces operations for which he had been awarded several medals for outstanding bravery under fire, amongst others. On his last mission, he had severely damaged his knee and had decided he was probably pushing his luck not to have suffered a more serious fate as had some of his fellow comrades, so he had resigned two years ago with a reasonable pension. Together with a third share of his now deceased father's estate, his mother having died some years earlier, he was comfortably well off, albeit not rich. Several of his investments had done well, which again helped to add to his overall income ensuring that he would not have to work again unless he chose too.

He had married Lydia about the time he joined the army when she was 20. Two years later, Jason was born and then Natasha six years after that, just before he had joined the special forces team. After that, it was one trip after another, sometimes being away for weeks at a time, even on more than one occasion, for several months.

Lydia was 47 but looked much younger, short neck length blonde hair turning slightly curly at the ends, 5' 2" with a very trim size 12 figure.

Natasha was the young, almost duplicate version of her mother, aged 19 with curves that drove all the boys she knew totally crazy. Honey blonde hair reaching down below her shoulders waving gently with the slight curls inherited from her as well. However, she did not suffer fools lightly as several had found out to their cost. She had been a bit tomboyish in her earlier years and was always ready for a bit of rough and tumble with the lads she had grown up with. Some had been at the receiving end of a fist if they had pushed it too far, she having been taught some basic self-defence by her father. She had been ill recently and was currently on leave from her university while she recovered.

Jason, on the other hand, while slightly taller than his father at 6' 2", light brown hair, slim but very fit and a body rapidly gaining muscular definition similar to his dad, the result of weight training and a passion for surfing. He had just been accepted as a trainer at the local surf school which is why he had joined his family to come to the new house. His ready cheeky smile, good looks and quick wit made him a target for every eligible female around.

"I never realised the house was so large. It did not look that big in the photos. Darling, it's huge and so many windows and gables. We are going to rattle around in that, so much so, we may have to use GPS!" exclaimed Lydia, laughingly.

Terry looked down at her and gave her a peck on the cheek with his lips.

"I never realised size mattered to you so much," he said with a slight smirk on his face. "Anyway, we had better drive down as I think it looks like the estate agent is already there to give us the keys. I also expect the furniture lorry will not be far behind. I asked the company to be punctual. Pile in guys and let's go."

They all entered the car, Terry sliding behind the wheel, starting the engine and slowly bounced down the uneven lane, gravel crunching beneath the tyres.

A white Ford Focus was parked outside the front door. As they stopped, the front door opened and a very attractive girl in her early 20s, high heels accentuating the firm curve of her calves, wearing a pale blue business suit, skirt stopping just above her knees, white blouse, almost see through but not quite but enough to see the shadow of her bra enclosing the swell of her breasts.

"Hi! You must be Mr Knight and family. I haven't been here long. I thought I might have been late. I'm Sophia. How lovely to meet you all. Mr Hargreaves couldn't make it so he asked me if I could greet you." This all came out in a rush. She caught sight of Jason getting out of the car and gave him a long look.

"Hi! Sophia. Nice to meetcha and thank you for coming over. It is a bit of a drive from the town," Terry drawled with a slight smile, eyes crinkling at the corners, having seen the sideways glance his son had given the young lady and having seen it all before.

"I have been briefed by Mr Hargreaves and I have all the keys here. Would you like me to give you a quick tour?"

"Yes, that will be great, although I don't think judging by the size of the house it is likely to be that quick. Just point out the basics and we will do the rest in due course. The van should be here shortly with some of our furniture and stuff and we want to get that unloaded while it is still light."

Sophia nodded her agreement. "If you would like to follow me," and led the way through the front doorway into the hall. Lydia wriggled her nose. "Doesn't smell too sweet, does it," she commented.

"It has been shut up for quite a time but I think that once you open the windows for a while it will be fine," Sophia explained.

The fairly modern windows clad with heavy metal shutters, belied the interior. Massive wooden beams crossed the ceiling supported by huge granite walls.

"Yay! Gods, the walls are seriously thick," Terry muttered. "They must be all of 4ft if not more. I wonder why they have placed those huge metal grills across the windows, bearing in mind the windows are fairly new. Just doesn't look quite right, somehow. Still everyone to their own taste, I suppose."

Numerous doorways opened out from the hall while in front of them was a wide polished wooden staircase which swept upstairs in a wide curve. They entered the first door and came into a large room, obviously designed to be a lounge with a tall wide fireplace on one side. Several more doorways opened away to other anterooms. They retraced their steps back to the hall, took another doorway and entered the kitchen. Surprisingly, a well laid out modern kitchen greeted them. There were plenty of storage cupboards, a built in American fridge-freezer, all the usual gadgets and to the delight of Lydia, an immense cooker with facilities for cooking with either gas or electric. Several doors ran off from the kitchen as well. A brief inspection showed it would take more time than was available to look at all of them. Back to the hallway and up the stairs. Sophia, heels clicking on the solid wooden planking, led the way.

In all, there were eight large bedrooms, six of them en-suite with two smaller rooms sharing another bathroom. There seemed to be some other rooms leading off the main landing. The oak beams, stained black with age continued the theme upstairs as well. There was a much smaller staircase leading higher again.

Just then a horn sounded outside. The furniture van had arrived. Three men got down from the cab and introduced themselves. Sophia gave Terry a large bunch of keys.

"I think the big ones are for the cellars. I have not been down as it is very dark and there seems to be something wrong with the lighting. I'm sure it can't be much. Sorry but I will have to go and get back to the office before it closes." Sophia swept her eyes over them, lingering on Jason just a little longer than necessary. "I'm sure I will see you all again soon and if you want anything, please, let me know, won't you?" With that, she jumped into the Focus, her skirt sliding up to reveal an extremely well-shaped thigh, much to Jason's obvious delight, revved the engine, spun the car round and shot up the drive, splashing gravel and dust everywhere.

"Well, come on, you guys, let's get stuck in and get this truck unloaded. Shouldn't take too long with all of us here!" Terry exclaimed.

With all the family helping the three men, they all worked with a will, Lydia directing operations, having allocated the bedrooms each were to use. Even so it was quite late before the task was completed and the autumn sun was slowly disappearing out to sea in the west, flecks of gold and pink touching the edges of the few clouds on the horizon.

"I hope the groceries arrive soon, otherwise we are going to go hungry and thirsty tonight," commented Terry.

"You did order them?" asked Lydia.

"Yes, of course."

Almost on cue, there was a rumble of tyres outside and a small van pulled up outside near the steps by the front door which was open. A small rotund, balding man wearing a black apron slid out from behind the driving wheel.

"I bet you thought I had forgot yer," addressing his remarks to nobody in particular. Jason went around to the back of the van with the man who opened the door to reveal a number of boxes inside.

"I'll help you," he said. In a few moments the boxes were safely dumped on the kitchen worktop with Lydia and Natasha busily unpacking the contents.

"Good Lord, we have enough to feed a small army. You have ordered just about everything, Terry."

Terry just smiled and pulling out his wallet, turned to the man and said, "I'll pay cash if that's all right. Would you like a cup of tea or something before you have to drive back?" he queried. "I assume this is your last delivery tonight?"

"Begging your pardon, Mister, I'll soon as be on my way." His eyes flickered around a little uneasily. "It do get dark around here mighty quick and I want to be away before then."

Terry frowned slightly. "You worried that you might get lost?" he asked.

"It's not a matter of getting lost. It's not a good place to be when dark do come," the man muttered.

Terry frowned again, "What do you mean?"

The man looked away at the gathering dusk. "Stories, maybe just stories but even so Mister, I'll be on my way. I do thank you kindly." And with that, he turned, jumped into his van, slammed the door and then carefully turned around and disappeared up the track.

"What do you make of that, Lydia?" Terry said.

"He did seem very nervous, didn't he?" she replied. "But maybe that is just his manner." She turned and went back inside to get cooking the meal. "Dinner in half an hour. OK!"

Terry gazed back up the track with a thoughtful look on his face and then followed his wife. They were all hungry and tired, what with the journey down from up country and with working hard to pack away all the furnishings which had arrived. They all agreed to finish the emptying of the remaining boxes for tomorrow. Pork chops, carrots, peas, boiled potatoes and some apple sauce were quickly consumed washed down with a generous glass of Pinot Grigio.

"That was good," Jason murmured, "but if you don't mind, I'm off to bed."

"Natasha and I have made up the beds," Lydia said, "sleep tight."

"Me too, Mum." Natasha bent down and kissed her cheek and then moved across to her father, gave him a tight hug. "Thanks for bringing me here, Dad! I think I'm going to love it."

She disappeared through the kitchen door and they could hear her going up the stairs.

"How about you, then?" Lydia asked.

"Why not?" Terry replied. Twinning fingers, they went first to lock the front door and then moved up the stairs to one of the master bedrooms, switching off the lights as they went.

Terry moved to the window and looked out. “It’s as black as Hades out there and there is not a single light to be seen. We do seem to be a bit isolated. I hope it is not too much.”

Lydia slid her arms around him. “It’s fine,” she whispered.

“I think I will go into town tomorrow and have a word with that estate agent guy, what’s his name? Erm, Hargreaves, that’s it,” Terry stated. “Goodnight, my darling.”

Tomorrow was another day.

* * * * *

Chapter Two
Stories

The following morning dawned fine and bright, the late Autumn sunshine shone on the front of the house making the granite blocks twinkle like diamonds with the early morning dew sparkling on the grass. They were all up and about and after a light breakfast, Terry turned to his family and confirmed his intention to go to town. "Would anyone like to come with me?" he asked.

"I'll come," said Jason, moving towards the door. Lydia looked at Terry.

"Natasha and I will clean up the house. It looks like a bomb has gone off in here. I really need to see if we can get rid of this terrible smell. I wonder if it could be the drains? Is the phone connected yet?"

Terry turned and as he went out of the door following Jason and said, "I'll try and sort it. The phone might take a day or two. There is no signal on my mobile, so I'll find out about that as well. I'll have a word with Hargreaves."

Half an hour later, they walked into Mr Hargreaves office. It had been easy enough to find as there were not too many shops or offices along the main street. In fact, the town looked a bit run down and most of the buildings seemed in dire need of a good decorating. A few people were wandering around with some striding along the pavement, obviously on an errand or so. A large sign hanging out over the office, swinging gently in the breeze, proclaimed to all this was indeed the office of J.D. Hargreaves Estate Agent.

John Desmond Hargreaves looked up from his desk as the newcomers entered and raising his not inconsiderable bulk out of his chair. Of florid complexion and all of 22 stone, he extended a hand with rather podgy fingers, shaking Terry's and Jason's in turn. He wore a dark grey suit which appeared to have been made for someone several sizes smaller with the buttons hanging on by threads across his rather large chest and stomach.

"How nice to see you again, Mr Knight and I take it that this is your son Jason?" Not waiting for a reply, he pressed on. "Hope everything is good at the house, I was fully reported to by my assistant, Sophia, no doubt she will be back shortly. I sent her on another job for me. She will be pleased to see you." His eyes paused as he looked over at Jason. "Please, take a seat. Anyway, how can I help you?"

"Well," said Terry. "It's like this. I would like to get a little more background information on the house. As you know everything was done in such a rush as we wanted to get the deal done as quickly as possible to make sure we didn't miss what had to be the sale of the century. Also, we need to get a landline in as soon as possible because our mobiles don't seem to work out there. I had thought there already was a line to the house but that doesn't seem to be the case."

"Just so, just so! Well, I'm afraid it is like this. Not enough mobile aerials and even if the one they have promised us is put up, there is no guarantee that you would get any reception anyway as you are so low down, set between the hills like you are. The landline, well, that's another matter. They are working on it but you are a bit, shall we say, erm, out of it. I'm sure you will have it soon, maybe in a week or two." He pursed his lips and smiled. "On the matter of the house, I can help you with a little information. Trelease House was owned and built by Sir Richard Trelease, some 300 years ago from the considerable fortune he had built up from the local mines he owned. He went to a great deal of trouble to build it, bringing in a team of master granite builders and quarrying the granite blocks from the quarry he also owned. The whole thing must have been a huge job. The actual construction is massive."

"It doesn't look as old as that but the house certainly is big," Terry interjected.

"Oh! But, it is. You have to remember the last owner, a direct relation, I think his name was Harvey Trelease, having been left it as it was passed down through the family and the ages, did a huge amount of restoration work, new windows and doors, even a new roof. That's real Delabole slate on that roof. Very difficult to get quantities like that now, especially as he wanted the old style to fit with the overall look, I suppose. All of this was done quite a long time ago, certainly before my time here." He paused for breath. "He was quite a young man, apparently, when he started on the restoration."

"Must have cost a packet! How did he fund it? Do you know?"

"The family have always been wealthy and I think he had a very good job. I'm not sure what he actually did but money never seemed a problem for him. Funny thing that! Thinking about it! He was always at home."

"Why so cheap then?" Terry asked.

Mr Hargreaves coughed nervously. "Well, it appears that he did not have any family, so to speak and the person he left it too, just a very good friend, I think, didn't want it. He just wanted the money as quick as he could. Rather undue haste in my opinion. Could have sold it for a lot more given time. It was a bit strange though as he spent quite a bit of money on it when he first moved in. New kitchen and central heating amongst others things. Then all of a sudden, he ups and wants to sell it right quick. It has been empty for quite a while ever since he moved out."

Mr Hargreaves looked at Terry somewhat quizzically.

"You strike me that you must have been a military man. Am I right?"

Terry looked at the ceiling for a second. "Yes, I was in the army."

"Oh, I am correct then. May I ask what branch?"

"Just the usual, you know, old boring stuff. Nothing too exciting, I'm afraid," Terry replied noncommittally.

"Ah! I see," said Hargreaves, frowning slightly. "Undercover stuff and the like, eh?" And gave a short laugh.

Terry ignored the comment and pressed on.

"So, Harvey Trelease is dead then?" Terry continued.

"Oh! Yes, dead, yes, dead." Mr Hargreaves stared at the ceiling and a bead of perspiration ran down his face, which was quickly mopped away with a large floral hanky.

"Recently?"

"Well, let me see, just over 20 years ago, I suppose. Time goes by so quickly. It was empty for quite a few years. Shame really being such a lovely old house."

"Was he ill for long?"

"No. It was very sudden. A bad fall, I believe. Dr Jackson tried to revive him at the house but without success. He reckoned he was dead almost instantly. Terrible business!"

"So the new owner, the one who was left it, never actually lived there?" Terry pressed.

"Err, yes, he did for a short while but I don't think it suited him being so isolated. Didn't like the air either or something, so he told me. Strange fellow, you know." He paused for breath again.

"So what was he like?"

"Oh, I never actually met him. He did everything generally by email and occasionally by phone and then left much of the other things to his solicitor who had power of attorney."

"Oh! Who was that?"

"A local chap. Does quite a bit of work for me, you know, legal stuff and all that. He goes by the name of Ho Sing. I am sure you will meet him sometime. He is also the local coroner."

"Do you know if the drains are OK? When we arrived, there was a terrible smell. Just wondered if it could be that the drains need cleaning out or maybe the septic tank needs emptying?"

Mr Hargreaves gave them both a long look. "Maybe, maybe. I can get a firm to check it out if you wish?"

"Yeah, great, thank you, as soon as you can if you could. I think we have taken up enough of your time, Mr Hargreaves. Thanks for all the info. I need to get on the doctors list here. I expect you have one?"

"Oh! Indeed, Doctor Jackson, down the street, turn left and the surgery is on your right. If I can help you with anything, please, just ask."

"That's great. I will get on it now." Terry and Jason said their goodbyes and exited the office. As they were crossing the road, a voice called to them. Sophia had just parked up and was coming towards them, greeting them with a big smile.

"How lovely! Nearly missed you. Been to see John? Hearts in the right place but needs to modernise things. Still, he does try and I think the world of him."

"I am off to the surgery to sign us up. Jason, why not take Sophia for a coffee or something while I'm doing that? There must be a cafe here somewhere." Terry winked at Jason, making sure that Sophia didn't see it.

"It is nearly my lunch hour, so that will be super. Mrs Winston's tea room is just around the corner," she said. "She's a good friend of mine."

"Meet you there shortly, then," Terry replied.

30 minutes later, Terry was back at the tea rooms. Jason and Sophia were at a table next to the window in deep conversation as Terry pulled up a chair and sat down. A grey-haired lady with a worn look on her face, rather rounded shoulders and wearing a little white piny around her waist came over to the table. Her face broke into a smile as she looked at Terry. "An' you must be Mr Knight, so very pleased to meet you. Sophia has told me all about you and your family. She be almost like a daughter to me seeing as I lost mine some 20 years ago." She looked down fondly at Sophia. "Don't know what I would do without her." Turning again to Terry. "Would'ee like something tea, coffee, maybe with one of my special homemade cherry buns?"

"Coffee, white, please, and a bun and very nice to meet you too." Terry smiled back. She bustled away. Jason looked at his father. "How did you get on?"

"Yes, fine, all done. I met Doctor Jackson himself. Bit of a strange guy, I thought. In fact, very strange. When I introduced myself and told him we had just bought Trelease House, the look he gave me was very peculiar. Then, just as I was going, he said something even stranger. "Don't go out alone at night near the marsh or the cliffs," he said. "It's very dangerous." When I asked him what he meant, he just clammed up and said goodbye. Most peculiar."

"Well," said Sophia. "I know the marsh has a bad reputation as you could get lost, especially at night as the paths would be difficult to follow and they sometimes change and become bogs. There have been rumours of strange things happening, probably old wives tales." She gave a little laugh. "But, I mean, no one in their right mind would go wandering out there at night. That's what he probably meant."

"Hmmm! I'm not convinced. It was the way he said it. Oh, well, maybe it's my army training that makes me suspicious. You're probably right!" Terry exclaimed.

"Dad, would it be OK if Sophia came over on Sunday for lunch as I still have a few days before I have to start work? As most of the tourists have gone and it's the end of the training season, I think I will be in the shop for a while to start with. They want me to organise training courses and theme days and put them on their web site well in advance of next year hoping for bookings for next season."

"I'm sure my wife and Natasha would love some company, especially if you can bring us up to speed on local things. Come on over whenever you like. We normally eat at about 1 o'clock. Roast chicken, I think, OK with you?"

Sophia looked at her watch. "Gosh, I must go or I will get the sack. Lovely, see you on Sunday, then." With that, she jumped up, lightly brushing Jason's shoulder with her finger tips as she passed, waved goodbye to Mrs Winston and disappeared out through the doorway.

Terry looked at his son with a big grin, "You are a fast worker, you randy little devil. I have to say she is rather stunning."

Jason just sniffed as they paid their bill and left Mrs Winston to her chores. A while later, they arrived back at the house to find virtually all the windows wide open with Lydia and Natasha busy washing and polishing the glass. Almost immediately, a tanker rumbled down the drive and pulled up outside the house. A sign with 'Clearway' emblazoned on its side gave it its purpose.

"You Mr Knight?" the driver asked.

"Good Lord, that was fast. I haven't long left Mr Hargreaves. He said he would sort it but I didn't expect you quite so quickly."

"Well, I was up the road a ways when he rang the office and they contacted me on the radio. Said it was urgent," the driver said, peering down from his cab.

"There is a terrible smell coming from somewhere, so we thought it might be the drains as we have only just moved in and the property has been empty for so long," Terry stated.

"If it be them, I'll be soon sorting it," he said, leaping out of the cab.

"Thanks, we will leave you to it. Can you check out the septic tank as well?" Terry asked.

"Just leave it to me my 'ansome." With that, he busied himself with unloading pipes and connecting them up to the tanker. About an-hour-and-a-half later, there was a tap at the door. "All done," he said. "But got a problems." He pushed his rather greasy looking cap to the back of his head, scratching his hair as he did so. "Couldn't be finding the septic tank. Looked everywhere for it. I be sure you ain't got one. Cleaned out all the traps, showered out them pipes but ain't find no tank."

Terry looked surprised. "Where does it go then?"

"Well, that be the mystery o' it. Them pipes, all seem to disappear into t'ground. It be very vexing." He coughed, bringing up some phlegm into his mouth, looked around for somewhere to spit it out, thought better of it and swallowed hard.

"You're right there, right vexing," Terry commented with a wry smile. The driver looked at him, obviously wondering if he was making fun of him.

"I'll be on my way then, bill will follow." With that, he swung up into his cab, started to up the tanker and with the engine roaring, bounced away up the drive.

Jason brought the girls up to speed about meeting Sophia, the Sunday lunch and the meeting with Mr Hargreaves, the lack of phones and his dad's comments on the Doctor. "How very sad about Mrs Winston's daughter, Wendy. Apparently, she went for a walk one day and just never came back. About 20 years ago it happened. The girl must have been about your age, Nat. The poor woman was distraught, particularly as her husband had died from a heart attack only a couple of months prior. They had most of the town out looking for her for days.

Eventually, they reckoned she must have fallen off the cliff into the sea but they never found a body."

"How awful." Gasped Lydia. Terry looked thoughtful but said nothing.

The two men went outside and went to work on the garden, which was a bit overgrown. It was evident that nothing had been done to keep it in order for a considerable time. They worked with a will and soon had a large pile of rubbish piled up which they then set light to. Thick smoke belched up from the fire and curled into the sky.

"I thought we might have stumbled onto the trap for the septic tank doing all this," Terry commented and wiping a hand across his face, gave Jason a slap on his back and said, "Come on, I think we have done enough for today. Let's get in and have a pint and then dinner."

He stepped backwards and suddenly his foot disappeared into a hole as the ground under him gave way. He toppled over to land on his back. "What the hell!" He exclaimed. He pulled his foot out and grimaced. It was covered in a brown slime up to his knee. Jason burst out laughing.

"I think you have found the tank, Dad," he said through chuckles. "God, you stink."

Terry looked down at the hole where the remains of some rotten planks were visible.

"Well, this is obviously not the cause of the fug in the house!" Terry exclaimed.

"I had better wash this sludge off before dinner, otherwise your mum will have a fit."

Terry stood up, both laughing at his misfortune. With that, they walked away, still smiling.

* * * * *

Terry didn't know what had woken him but he felt that something must have as he normally slept soundly. He lay quietly, listening intently but the only sound he could hear was Lydia breathing next to him, her arm wrapped around a pillow, the blonde strands of her hair splaying out around her head.

Very slowly and quietly, he slid out of bed, totally naked and padded across to the window which was open. Moonlight spilt through the opening and as he looked out, he could see the valley beyond partially illuminated. Mist trailed across it, looking like tendrils of smoke obscuring the lower part where the marsh was. It was a very peaceful and tranquil view and, in the sky, a few stars were visible. Terry took a deep breath, stretched and turned to return to bed, rubbing his eyes as he did. Suddenly, he stiffened, all senses alert, swinging around to face the window again. A low resonant moan echoed across the valley. It was such a melancholy sound but so full of menace. Terry's hairs on his arms and back of his neck prickled. It stopped almost as soon as it had started, so suddenly that Terry thought he had imagined it. He stared out of the window but nothing moved. A whisper of wind ruffled the bushes and trees. He was about to turn away when it was repeated this time nearer, louder and for longer. He waited. A small droplet of perspiration formed on his forehead and slowly ran down the side of his face but he did not move a muscle, so intense was his concentration. Nothing! A few clouds slowly obscured the face of the moon and the valley darkened. Ten minutes trickled by. Terry stared into the darkness. What was that! On the far side of the garden, beyond the boundary wall, a thick growth of tall conifers grew, waving gently in the lightest of breezes. He wiped his eyes and looked again. Shadows moved, waxing and waning in the faint silver light. Is one of the shadows more than a shadow? More solid? Something! A figure? Was it there earlier or was he just imagining it? A breeze stirred the branches of the trees again, rustling the pine needles with a soft whispering noise. He rubbed his eyes again, cursing under his breath to himself his sleepiness. He had an overwhelming sense of someone looking at him. Call it an intuition from the old days of his missions into enemy territory. The moon brightened the scene as it emerged from behind a cloud and the shadow disappeared. Had he imagined it? He shook his head with annoyance. He strained every sense, wondering what, if anything he had seen or not. Then, far away, the sound echoed again around the valley but so much fainter that Terry had to strain his ears to hear it.

"What are you doing?"

Terry started visibly and looked around at Lydia, who was sitting up in the bed, sheet having fallen to her waist, exposing her firm, naked breasts.

"Sorry if I woke you but I heard a noise and was looking out of the window to see if I could see what it was."

"Come on, back to bed. You'll catch your death of cold standing there without anything on."

Terry slid back between the sheets, instantly feeling the familiar and musky smell of his naked wife. She wriggled around so her back was towards him and gently rotated her pert posterior up against his groin.

"Mmmm! That feels so good," she whispered as she felt him rising up behind her. He ran his hand down over her shoulder and curled it around her tight breast, feeling the nipple hardening in the palm of his hand. She slowly spread her thighs as he probed between them, his hips gently thrusting towards her. She gave a little gasp and then a sigh of contentment as he slivered into her wetness and then he gave a groan himself as he thrust harder, grinding his groin against her silky flesh. It was all over very quickly, she feeling the flooding of her body, both panting slightly with the intense experience. He kissed her back, so very gently, almost reverently. Within minutes, they were both sound asleep, curled together.

*****

Chapter Three
Sunday

Lydia was first down in the morning and immediately got to work preparing breakfast. Natasha was next to appear but looked tired.

"Are you all right, my darling?" Lydia asked, looking concerned.

Natasha yawned loudly. "I'm just tired, Mum. Kept waking up. I'm not sleeping too well at the moment."

"Why do you think that is, then?"

"Don't really know. Just noises in the night."

"Noises? Here? You probably have been having a nightmare. They can seem very real at times. But, noises, come on, sweetie, this place has got to be the least likely place in the country to suffer from night noise."

"Well, maybe but something is waking me up and I am fed up with it."

"I think your dad and I are going to go into town later this afternoon, so take some paracetamol, get your head done and catch up with a few zizzes while there is no one to disturb you. It will do you good, I'm sure. Good idea or no?"

Natasha looked at her mum and smiled. "Good idea."

Terry sauntered into the kitchen and looked around. "Good morning, folks."

"Where's Jason? Is he awake?" Lydia asked.

"Are you kidding me? I think he has been up since dawn, scrubbing up. He has spent more time in his bathroom this morning than Natasha does when she's on a night out. You can practically smell the after shave lotion from here." He laughed.

They settled in around the table and had practically finished their light breakfast when Jason eventually appeared.

"Going somewhere, Jason?" His dad inquired innocently.

Jason looked at him and refused to be drawn.

"I think he wants to make an impression. I don't think there is anything wrong with that. You go for it, my boy. I sometimes wish other people would make that sort of effort for me," said Lydia, looking over at Terry. He just grinned.

"Have you been messing about in my bedroom, Jason?" Natasha asked a little angrily.

Jason looked at her, frowning slightly. "What do you mean?"

"Some of my stuff has been moved."

"So I did it?" Jason was now getting annoyed.

"Well, you often used to rummage around in my room when I was younger, just to be a nuisance. You used to think it funny."

"It's not funny that you accuse me. I haven't even been in your room, so the answer, Natasha, is no!!!"

Natasha was not impressed. "My stuff has been moved. I am not making it up!"

"Come on, guys, I'm sure there is a reasonable explanation, so, please, calm down, both of you," said Lydia.

Both Natasha and Jason looked unhappy but the argument was over, at least for the time.

Terry wandered out into the garden and ambled over to where the conifers grew. He looked around intently, turning his head towards the house and in particular to the window of his bedroom. "Yes, it must have been near here," he muttered to himself as he lined up what his view of this area would have been from upstairs.

He walked up to the trees and looked around again, inspecting the ground. There! Beside the largest of the pines, the undergrowth was all flattened alongside it. He bent down and ran his hand over the grass. Something had stood there recently. He had not imagined it and his eyes had not played tricks on him. He scratched his head uncertainly. He tried to think what could it have been but nothing sprang to mind. Person or animal? Bending over, he sniffed the ground and detected a faint and slightly acidic scent which he could not identify. He stood up and then noticed that there was some torn bark on the side of the tree, just over shoulder height. Four short strips and obviously recent. Sap was still exuding from the wounds. Terry pursed his lips. He raised his hand to touch the strips and realised immediately that whatever made the marks must have been considerably taller than he was as he had to stretch up to touch them. It didn't make any sense. He walked slowly back to the house and join the rest of his family.

The morning rushed by and there was a sound outside of a car pulling up. Jason was first to the door and flung it open to reveal Sophia coming up the steps. She wore a frilly white blouse, sparkly tight jeans and pink trainers, hair tied back into a ponytail completed the attractive look.

"Wow! You look great," Jason exclaimed. He moved in closer, brushing his lips across her offered cheek. "You also smell gorgeous as well."

"Thank you, kind sir." She smiled back. "You don't look so bad yourself." Her eyes sparkled and she flushed slightly.

They walked back into the kitchen and Sophia placed a couple of bottles of wine on the table. "Hope you will like these. How good to see you all again."

"Lunch will be in about an hour, so go and find something to do while Natasha and I get things ready," said Lydia. "Natasha, be a darling and lay up the table for me, will you?"

"Sure thing, Mum."

"I'm going to take Sophia around the garden and show her the work Dad and I did yesterday," said Jason and taking Sophia by the hand, disappeared outside.

Terry looked at the girls and picked up his flashlight and the bunch of house keys. "I'm going to have a look at the cellar and try and see what I need to do to get power on down there."

"I'll give you a shout when lunch is ready," said Lydia.

With that, he went out into the hall and down the corridor to a door set back into the wall. Terry tried the handle. It didn't move. He looked at the keys in his hand and selected the largest of them and inserted it in lock. It turned easily enough. He tried the handle again and with much creaking and protesting, he slowly pushed the heavy door open. A strange musty smell assailed his nostrils. He wrinkled up his nose in disgust. There was a light switch on the wall which he tried to no effect and so he flicked on the flashlight and shone it around. A very heavy duty armoured electric cable was fixed to the ceiling. Within a few feet of the doorway, there was a stairway leading sharply downwards built out of huge granite slabs. Terry moved forward and started to descend, taking care not to slip on the slightly uneven surface. Within a few moments, all natural light from the doorway disappeared and he continued down the spiral steps. Luckily, there was a thick rope threaded through some old iron spikes set into the wall which helped him as he headed into the unknown.

Ye Gods, I must be 40 feet down at least, he mused. He stopped for a moment and switched off the flashlight. The darkness was total. Even after a few seconds of keeping his eyes closed to help his sight acclimatise to the blackness, he still could not see anything at all. He switched on the light again and continued down. Suddenly, the steps came to an end and he stepped into low tunnel about 20 feet long with another large door at the far end. As he approached it, he noticed that the door was of massive construction with huge hinges but much to his surprise, fixed to the top and bottom of the door were two heavy bolts. *Now why would someone fix them there? That is to keep someone IN not OUT. How very strange,* he thought. He slid the bolts back, which to his surprise needed very little effort, even though they were of extremely large construction. He inspected them closely and realised they were covered in thick grease and had been installed very precisely. The door was another matter as it obviously hadn't been opened in a long time. Terry heaved at the handle ring and very reluctantly, the big door slowly swung open. He looked at the door again and was surprised to notice a number of long gashes on the inside of the wood. He ran his fingers over them, trying to work out what could have made such deep, long scratches. The smell, which Terry had noticed upstairs, was now much stronger, oppressive with chemical overtones. It made him gag slightly but it did not prevent him from entering the room beyond. He swung the flashlight around and stopped with amazement. The room was huge, even though the ceiling was quite low. He estimated that it must be over 60 feet long and probably thirt30y feet wide but that was not what held his gaze. Lined up along both walls and again through the centre of the room were long steel tables packed with laboratory equipment of all types. Trays full of glass phials, retorts, heaters, pipes, machines of all sizes and types, the purpose for which Terry couldn't even guess lined the tables as far as he could see. Computers with their accompanied screens, keyboards and cables were in a long row down one side. Some large round vats were fixed to the floor at the far end of the room. Pipes connected some of them together in a confused tangle.

Terry walked slowly down the rows, examining this and that with increasing curiosity. A crunch of broken glass under his shoes stopped him in his tracts. He swung the flashlight over the floor and noticed for the first time that it was strewn with debris presumably from the nearest table. Machines had been torn from mounts and electrical sockets together with some computer towers and monitors. Glass retorts and phials were littered all around mostly smashed but with some having survived and still containing some various fluids. Cables cascaded from the table and lay in jumbled piles across the floor. Something traumatic had obviously happened within this area but what? That was what was going through Terry's mind. His attention was suddenly caught by a part of a small photo protruding from behind a computer screen. He bent down and gently prised it free from beneath all the debris. He shook the dust off it. It was of two young men in white coats

– one with his hand resting on the shoulder of the shorter and one who had a short goatee beard. Part of the picture was missing and there was some writing on the back but Terry could not read what it said, especially in the bad light. He looked around the cavern and noticed a large electrical fuse box fitted to a wall at the far end. He made his way to it and pressed the catch. The lid flipped open exposing long lines of circuit breakers. He shone the light over them. Most of the switches were in the 'off' position. Flicking the off ones to on, he press the main breaker switch. Something fizzed in the breaker and then nothing. Something somewhere was shorting out. Terry looked at his watch and suddenly realised he was already late for lunch. He carefully made his back to the doorway and closing the door behind him, climbed back up the steps, carefully closed the door at the top, relocking it as he did so. As he re-entered the kitchen, Lydia looked up. "Hi! Thought we had lost you down there. I did shout but couldn't hear you."

Terry grinned as he sat down at the table. "I'm not surprised I couldn't hear you. That cellar is vast and very deep. You will not believe what is down there. Only a full blown laboratory but there is more. Something happened down there. A section of it is smashed to hell and back. I did find this though." He pulled out the scrap of photo and let them inspect it. "Do you recognise either of the men, Sophia?" Terry asked.

She looked at it very carefully. "The only thing I can see is that it looks quite old and…oh! Look, there is some faint writing on the back, looks like in pencil." She screwed up her eyes in concentration. "P_O_R_T. I can't make out the rest, it's too faint."

"Well done," said Terry and looked pleased. "I will get a magnifying glass on it in due course. In the meantime, let's eat. I'm starving!"

The meal was consumed amid considerable laughter and good humour.

"We are going into town this afternoon. Natasha is going for a sleep, so what are you two going to get up too?" Terry inquired looking at Jason and Sophia.

Jason looked at his dad. "I think Sophia is going to show me the cliffs, you know, the way to the coastal path, especially as the weather looks good."

Terry frowned slightly. "The forecast is not so good for later. In fact, I think I heard them say there was a yellow warning out for this evening. Big storm coming so they said."

"We will be fine, Dad. We should be back before that comes in. Come on, Sophia, let's go and explore."

"Thanks for a lovely lunch, Mrs Knight," said Sophia.

They went out and around to the back of the house and joined the track towards the river. The sun was shining with a light westerly breeze and for the time of the year, it felt quite warm and Jason and Sophia crossed the little bridge arm in arm. They smiled at each other and Jason pulled her towards him and gently kissed her on the lips. Sophia did not resist and stopped for a moment, sliding her arms around his neck. Both of them then laughed and still laughing entered the woods. It was gloomy beneath the trees with the occasional flash of dappled sunlight breaking through the waving branches, leaves beginning to flutter to the ground rustling around their feet, a silent reminder that autumn was on its way and that summer was nearly over. The trees thinned out, the path skirting the mine spoil and eventually joined the wider cliff path.

"Wow! What a view!" Jason exclaimed. The sea, 200 feet below them shimmered in the late afternoon sun. The swells roared in to the rocks, giving up their power in a magnificent display of white foam which was blasted high into the air before falling again to re-join the blue green sea. Gulls of various types swirled and wheeled in the up-draught, calling to one another. In the distance, a long line of black cloud obscured the horizon, looked ominous.

"I think Dad may be right about the weather changing. That looks like the beginning of the storm front which is forecast."

Sophia nodded in agreement. "I think you are correct. Come on, I want to show you something." Taking Jason by the hand, she led the way towards the edge of the cliffs. There was a small dip in the ground with the surrounding ground covered in thick soft grass and tufts of thrift. It was a natural amphitheatre. She sat down, drawing Jason down beside her. She lay back, resting her head on the grass. "Look how peaceful it is up here. The sound of the sea, the birds, the buzzing of the insects, even the sound of the sheep in the distance."

They watched as a buzzard wheeled around on the thermal air currents, high above them, occasionally mewing with its instantly recognisable call.

"It's beautiful," Jason murmured. "Just like you."

Sophia flashed her eyes. "Thank you, kind sir. You are not so bad yourself."

Jason slid his arm around her shoulders and drew her close to him. She tilted her head and their lips meshed in a passionate, lingering, embrace. Time passed. Jason felt himself getting aroused. He slowly moved his hand to the top button of her blouse, brushing the fullness of her firm breasts. He felt her stiffen suddenly and then she pushed him away with a gasp, her arm outstretched, finger pointing. Jason over balanced and rolled away from her. "What the hell!" And then again "What the hell!" as he followed the direction of finger.

A man was standing on the top of the hillock just above and behind them. He wore a camouflage suit, very worn and fraying at the edges, heavy boots with thick cleated soles, an old floppy hat covered his head where wisps on long grey hair mingled with the tousled beard around his face. What held Jason's attention even more was the well-oiled, wicked looking shotgun he had slung under his arm. From the casual way he held it, Jason could see he was obviously completely at ease with it.

"I don't know who the hell you are or what you want but point that bloody gun away from us." Jason raged. "What do you think you are doing frightening us like that?"

"Begging your pardon, young sir. I had no wish to frighten' ee. I own the sheep up 'ere and I be missing one. I fancied I saw ee when I see a flash of white in the distance but all the time it were this young ladies top. My name is 'arry Welford. I believe I know Miss Sophia ''ere. An' who might ee be?" the man inquired.

"I'm Jason Knight and I've just moved in to Trelease House."

"Bit young to be the master of that," he said, his lip curling unpleasantly.

"My dad has bought it. I'm his son!"

"Oh, ay! I heard tell someone had moved in to the old place. 'bout time someone did. Too good a place to leave empty. Sorry, young fella, I meant no offence."

"Apology accepted," Jason said, somewhat mollified. "I'm sorry too. I mean we haven't seen your sheep."

"Bleddy dogs, that's what it be. Bleddy dogs. They come up from the town and chase the sheep 'till they kill ee. Found one only the other day, been chased right off the cliff edge. Could see the body on a ledge hundred feet down. Folks don't realise the trouble some of their bleddy dogs cause to hard working fellas like me." Harry sucked at his teeth. "Still, I'll be catching them one day and then it'll be another story."

"You mean you'll shoot them?" Jason looked uncomfortable.

"Too bleddy right, I'll shoot 'em! I don't miss much when I be firing! Used to be quite a sharp shooter when I be younger an' this being a pump action repeater. They be illegal now, I believe." Harry chuckled at his own joke. "Anyway, you good people best be on your way if you are not to get wet." He tilted head in the direction of the sea. Jason looked around and realised that while they had been talking, the weather had changed dramatically. The wind had risen appreciably, dark, scudding clouds were rapidly obscuring the sun and then, suddenly, in the distance, a flicker of lightening.

"We are on our way. Come up to the house sometime for a coffee. Dad will like to meet you, I'm sure." Jason invited.

"Coffee is it? I no drank no bleddy coffee in years but I'll have a proper drink with your dad if ee so asks." Harry gave Jason a broad wink.

"I'm sure that could be arranged." Jason smiled back.

Rain was just starting to fall as they turned and quickly made their way back along the coastal path.

"We better go back via the old mine house. It will be easier and closer," said Sophia. They came to an old stile which Jason climbed over and then stopped to look back the way they had come. He could still just see Harry still standing on the hillock. As he did so, he failed to see Sophia catch her foot in the top rung of the style and she fell heavily, just managing to fling out an arm to break her fall against Jason. She rolled over onto a clump of thickly growing bracken at the side of the style. Jason stooped to grab her. She lay there laughing up at him.

"That will teach me to be more careful in future." She stretched out her hand to help herself up and suddenly grimaced. Her hand slipped on something wet and sticky. She held it up to look at it and gave a little scream. Her hand was covered in blood. Jason rushed over to her and kicked the bracken to one side. He then helped Sophia to her feet.

"I think you have just found Harry's missing sheep." He looked back again and could still just see Harry in the distance. He gave a thrill whistle and saw Harry turn towards him. Jason waved his arms wildly and was relieved to see him start to jog towards them. In a few moments, Harry had joined them, amazingly, not even out of breath, bearing in mind his age.

"Yep, that is mine," he said and then coughed. He was obviously upset at the discovery of the carcass. "Looks like the throats been ripped right out. Bleddy dogs! I'm going to 'ave 'em this time. They will probably come back tonight for another meal."

Harry looked around. The rain was falling steadily now and the lightening was closer with a few murmurs of thunder audible above the sound of the surf.

"This path never done me any favours," he said.

"What do you mean?" said Jason.

"This be where I did find Minnie's old Man."

Jason looked perplexed. Sophia looked at Harry intently. "You mean Minnie Winston's husband?"

"The very same. He was almost dead when I did find ee. Not for long, I did reckon. Poor chap. He had tried to crawl a way along this path. Must have got struck down pretty quick if you ask me. Mud all over the front of his clothes. Front of 'is trousers ripped to hell. I'll never forget the look on 'is face, poor bugger, begging your pardon, Miss Sophia. He looked terrified. Not surprising really if you think about it, knowing ee wasn't going to make it. Ee tried to talk to me but I couldn't fathom what ee was saying. Gabbled on about a 'gargoyle' or sumint whatever that is. I think ee was just about out of his mind. I really didn't know what to do, so I stayed with ee 'til the end which was not long. Then I went to Trelease House to phone for help. Being the nearest, you understand. Luckily, Dr Jackson was at the house, so he came back with me. Was dark by the time we got back 'ere. Sorry. And me bringing all this up when I knows you be a great friend of Minnie. Anyways, you just leave this to me and I thank ee kindly. You get this girl to the dry. This storm is going to be a bad 'em."

Jason and Sophia left the old man and ran towards the old mine house which they could just see in the distance. As they arrived at the building, they took shelter for a few moments to get their breath back. The rain was now sluicing down in torrents and they were both soaked to the skin. It was getting darker by the minute and the lightening was flashing regularly with huge peals of thunder crashing about them. Jason peered around the corner of the wall and looked out to sea. There was no break in the clouds and if anything, they looked even more formidable. Just then a huge flash illuminated the sky and Jason noticed a small pointed headland to his right. About halfway down the cliff, there appeared to be a cave. It disappeared in the intense blackness after the lightening. Suddenly, another violent explosion of light. Jason wiped the rain from his eyes which was now pouring down his face in a steady stream. Was it his eyes playing tricks on him or did he really see something move in the dark aperture of the cave? A huge explosion of surf spewed into the air completely shrouding the headland from view. Jason recoiled. A low moaning sound reverberated around the bay quickly being lost in the tumult of other sounds.

"What in God's name was that?" he exclaimed, the hairs at the back of his neck starting to tingle.

Sophia was now shivering with the dramatic drop in temperature and her soaked clothes. "A seal calling, perhaps."

"I have never heard a seal make a noise like that. Oh! Baby, I'm sorry, you are freezing. Come on, let's run for it again. Not too far to go now." Hand in hand, they scrambled along the path until it forked away towards Trelease House. Panting, they hurried across the bridge and on to the last lap towards the house. Staggering now and completely out of breath, they gratefully walked up the steps to the front door and swung it open. Jason tried the light switch but nothing happened. He search around, fumbling in the almost total darkness and then gave a grunt of satisfaction. He flicked on his dad's flashlight and shone it around.

"Dad and Mum are still out 'cause the car not here," he stated. "Come on, my girl, upstairs and get a hot shower before you catch your death of cold. You can use my room and I will check on Natasha to make sure she is OK. I'll get a shower in one of the other bathrooms. Make yourself at home." With that, Jason led the way up the stairs and left Sophia at the door of his bathroom. He then went out and along the hallway to Natasha's room. He peeped inside and with the flashlight beam set to one side, saw his sister fast asleep on her bed. A half glass of water and a packet of pills on the bedside table told its own story. He backed quietly out and closed the door very carefully. He then retreated back down the corridor and entered one of the spare rooms. He stripped of his sodden clothing and left them in a pile on the tiles and stepping into the shower cubicle, switched on the taps, revelling in the hot water as it coursed over his body. Slowly, the feeling started to return to his hands and feet. When he felt thoroughly warmed up, he flipped off the tap, found a large fluffy towel which he vigorously dried himself with, before rapping it around his waist and leaving the bathroom, made his way back to his own room. Lightening flickered, illuminating the corridor for a split second. Almost immediately the thunder crashed virtually overhead. Jason flinched unintentionally. He made the doorway of his bedroom just as the battery of the flashlight started to dim. He entered the room and stopped abruptly. Sophia was standing in the centre beside the bed in his dressing gown. She looked at him for a moment and then with tantalising slowness in the failing light of the torch put her hands on the gowns tie and let it fall open. It was obvious to Jason she was completely naked underneath. He took a deep breath and without taking his eyes off her, slowly closed the door behind him. He moved towards her until he stood directly in front of her and gently hooked his forefingers into the collar of the gown either side of her neck, moving them outwards over her shoulders until it slid to the floor. Another flash of lightening played across the room, turning parts of her body to dark shadows while lighting others.

He held out his hand, which trembled slightly as he cupped one of her beautifully formed breasts in it. Then he did the same with the other hand. Her nipples were hard and tight against his fingers.

"God! But you are so gorgeous," he whispered into her ear before slowly nuzzling her neck with his lips. Sophia's hand slid down to Jason's waist and eased the towel away until that too slipped to the floor. Her other hand curled around the nape of his neck, finger tips digging into his flesh. Her lips kissed his ear and very slowly her tongue slithered into it. Jason shook with suppressed passion, his arms curling around the firm roundness of her buttocks and lifted her up into the air. Her thighs wrapped around his waist as he carried her to the edge of the bed.

"I want you so bad." He panted.

"I wanted you from the moment I first saw you," she replied.

Their bodies collapsed onto the mattress, Jason rolling over until he lay between Sophia's legs, now kissing her body with infinite patience, running his tongue down across her breasts, her nipples and then even more slowly down and down to the dark triangle at the top of her silky thighs. Sophia moaned with pleasure as she arched her body upwards towards Jason's straining body. He inhaled her subtle perfume as he stretched his body, straightening himself while supporting most of his weight on his elbows. His mouth found hers in the darkness, tongues entwining, his hips starting to gently thrust towards her. His manhood now fully aroused, found her and with complete gentleness, slid into her moistness, deeper and deeper he moved with Sophia returning his thrusting with equal enthusiasm. Her hands slid down his back until firmly gripping his tight buttocks, whereupon both of them rocked up and down more and more desperately, suddenly frantically, both panting, Jason grunting with exertion, Sophia moaning and suddenly crying out in total abandonment, legs thrashing in the air behind Jason and then as Jason partially withdrew and then thrust in deeply, grunting with desire until he could hold back no longer and uttering a harsh guttural cry. Oh! So deep that Sophia felt as if her whole being was on fire, met him with the same fierce up thrust as he filled her with his seed.

They lay there exhausted with their efforts, Jason trembling. Lightening flickered faintly in the distance. Thunder from it following it a while later, a shore sign the storm was at last moving away. The wind had also died down but the rain was still torrential. They lay side by side, holding hands, listening to the sound of the raindrops smashing against the window and roof until their breathing became back to normal.

"That was so wonderful, Jason."

"Oh! Sophia! You are magnificent. I think I am in love with you!"

Sophia wriggled slightly so she could cuddle up to him. "I hope you are! I Know I do. I don't do this with anyone, you know?"

They snuggled up together, eyes blinking to start with and then closing completely as sleep overcame them.

Then the screaming started!

* * * * *

Chapter Four
The Inn

When Terry and Lydia left the house, the sun was still shining but the dark clouds of the storm were gathering in the distance. Natasha had made her excuses and, as her mother had suggested, took some tablets to help her sleep and with a muttered, "See you later." went up to her room.

They drove to the town without any incident and parked up close to what looked like the principal Inn of the town.

Hanging baskets, still colourful with flowers, even this late in the season festooned the walls outside, almost covering the lead paned windows. A sign hung from the wall, creaking in the light breeze, proclaiming this to be 'The Red Fox Inn'.

"Looks old," said Terry. "Let's go in and see if the inside is as good as the outside."

He held the door open for Lydia to pass through and then followed her. A warm welcoming bar extended along part of the wall in front of them, expertly lit with hidden lighting. Horse brasses covered the low beams, all shining and polished with obvious care. More brass items hung from the walls and over the far side there was a huge open log fire blazing away merrily. A number of tables occupied the centre space with some more private cubicles along the remaining walls.

Several people were in the process of dining with a young girl attending the tables. She smiled as they caught her eye. A pleasant faced man in his early 40s peered at them from behind the bar. He had a very pronounced scar running across his forehead.

"Can I help you guys?" he asked. Then he grinned at Terry and then said in an undertone, "Hi, Boss!"

"Good Lord!" said Terry, obviously startled. "What in Heavens are you doing here?"

"I might just about ask you the same," he said, still smiling. "Although I already know the answer to that seeing that gossip flows like water in these parts."

Lydia looked puzzled. "You obviously know each other but…"

Terry turned to her and smiled. "Lydia, meet an old buddy of mine, Dave 'Bomber' Bates, last known address, Afghanistan."

"And now of The Red Fox Inn, which I bought when I left the army shortly after you had gone. I came down with my girlfriend over there." Nodding towards the young waitress who looked at them with a big smile.

"Di, this is my old boss, Terry Knight. You remember? I told you all about him?"

"Of course, I remember," Di replied, laughing. "Nice to meet you."

Dave turned to Lydia and said quietly, "I owe my life to your old man and I will never rest until I manage to repay him one day. He pulled me out when everyone else had bought it. We both ended up in hospital on that little jolly. They say I died twice on the operating table. I was still convalescing when he left. Never did manage to thank you properly, Boss."

Terry looked embarrassed. "Think nothing of it, Davy. All part of the job," he said gruffly. "Just make sure you don't talk about, especially around here."

"Wouldn't dream of it. Now what would you like to drink? On the house, of course."

"A pint of lager and a gin and tonic for my lady if you please. And, er, thank you," replied Terry.

Davy turned and served up the drinks. "I think someone has just sussed you over the other side. Mr Hargreaves, no less."

"We had better go over and talk to him. See you later, Davy." Terry raised his hand in recognition to Mr Hargreaves beckoning.

Together they walked over to the cubicle where he sat.

"Sit down, sit down. Oh! This must be your lovely wife. Pleased to meet you, Mrs Knight. This is Dr Jackson and his good friend, Ho Sing."

"Oh, just call me Lydia and please, don't get up. Good to meet you all."

Terry looked at them, nodded, placed their drinks on the table and then they both sat down. John Hargreaves motioned towards the bar. "You know Davy then?"

"Yes, we have met before," said Terry casually. "Although it was quite a long time ago."

Dr Jackson stared at him and then glanced over towards the bar where Davy was busy polishing some glasses.

"Ho is a lawyer here in town. He does most of my legal work and very good he is at doing it too. He is also our local coroner," explained John. "Dr Jackson, I think you already know."

"Yes, I do," said Terry. "Good to meet you, Ho. Where do you originally come from?"

Ho's face was impassive. "I came originally from Korea," he said with a slight accent tingeing his voice.

"North or South?" Terry inquired with a smile.

"South, of course."

"Yes, of course," Terry commented, slightly sarcastically.

Dr Jackson turned to him. "And how are you all settling in over at the house?"

"Yes, fine, thanks. Takes a bit of adjusting to the quiet but it is in a beautiful location," said Terry. "Found a few strange things though."

The three other men looked at one another. "Oh! Do tell us," said Dr Jackson a little sarcastically.

Terry looked around the table. "Well, there is the underground laboratory to start with and then there is the photo I found down there."

"What! Underground laboratory? Good Heavens! Really?" said John.

The other two looked at each other. "Photo, you said," said Dr Jackson. *He exchanged glances with Ho, a little nervously*, Terry thought to himself.

"Yes, this one." Terry pulled out the sliver of torn paper. "Anyone you know?" he asked innocently. They passed it around between themselves. One by one they shook their heads. "Not a good picture, is it? And quite old I would say." John mused as he inspected it. *Pity it is not complete.*

"Yes, I agree. Still, I thought I would ask. It's no big deal. I just was intrigued, especially with the writing on the back."

"Writing? What writing?" Dr Jackson's face was intense.

"P>O>R>T I think it says but I could be wrong. But like I said, it is of no importance," said Terry as he placed the photo carefully back into his pocket.

Dr Jackson and Ho exchanged glances again and then both stood up. "We must be off," said Dr Jackson. "You know surgery and all that."

"Yes, of course, you must be busy," said Terry coolly. "Nice to meet you Ho."

"Likewise, Terry, Mrs Knight, goodbye."

Once they had left, Terry turned to John. "Surgery? On a Sunday?"

"Oh! He must have forgotten what day it is. He seems in a world of his own these days. Oh, dear. There goes the electric!" John exclaimed. As they had been talking, the storm had suddenly arrived, violent flashes of lightening followed rapidly with the thunder. They could hear the rain smashing now against the leaded panes.

"Don't worry, folks," shouted Davy from the bar area. "I'll soon have it fixed." And sure enough a few moments later light from a number of candles illuminated the inn, making it feel even more cosy than it was previously with the electric lights.

Terry and Lydia downed their drinks and stood up. "We had better go as well, just in case it gets even worse," said Terry.

"Very wise, Terry," said John. "Just be very careful on the way back. The runoff from some of the hills crosses your road back and has been known to wash it completely away before now."

Terry and Lydia said cheerio and walked back past the bar where Davy was tidying up glasses.

"Come over and see us soon, Davy," said Terry. He looked around carefully to check nobody was within earshot and then said quietly, "I would really like to talk to you about recon."

Davy looked up at that and frowned. "Soon?"

"Yes, soon."

"Cheers."

As they hurried to their car, which luckily was parked close to the Inn, Lydia looked at Terry. "What was all that about?"

"Dunno! Call it intuition. There is something a bit strange about our friend Dr Jackson and maybe even this guy Ho."

They drove back very carefully. John had been right. The rain was still pounding down, even though the lightening appeared to be receding into the distance. The water was pouring through every gateway they passed. Mud and gravel, which had been washed out from the fields, made the road slippery and with the water now flooding the ditches made it difficult to actually follow the road. Eventually, they made it, turning in rather gratefully to the drive of the house and stopping as close as they could to the front door. Not a light was showing.

"The electric must be out here as well," Lydia commented.

They both jumped out and then both froze. Someone was screaming as if in mortal terror.

* * * * *

Chapter Five
Weird Things

Terry didn't hesitate and hurtled up to the door, which was unlocked, burst through it and charged up the stairs with Lydia close behind, heading towards where the screaming appeared to be coming from. As he ran down the corridor, all of a sudden a door opened almost beside him and a figure shot out of the doorway and collided with him. They both collapsed in a tangle of arms and legs and rolled over and over, grappling to get a hold. Within seconds, Terry had managed to roll on top of his assailant and put him in an arm lock. The figure let out a cry of pain and Terry immediately relaxed his hold. "Jason?"

"Dad?"

In the dark they hadn't been able to see who each other were. In the poor light, they looked around at Lydia. Another scream rent the air from farther down the corridor.

"Natasha," Lydia shouted and pushing Terry out of the way, frantically ran towards her bedroom. Reaching it, she flung the door open and even though it was still very dark, could just make out her daughter curled up on the bed. She rushed over to her and wrapped her arms around her. Natasha was shaking all over and was not able to speak at first, such was her terror. Terry and Jason crowded in behind them.

"Whatever is the matter, baby," Lydia whispered as her held her close. "Have you had a bad dream or something?"

Natasha whimpered in fear and her face was wet with tears. Eventually, she managed to whisper a reply, "Something was in my room. It touched me. Mum, please, don't let it hurt me."

"Of course, I won't, baby. You are safe now, whatever it was."

Terry touched Jason's arm. "Let's check out the house. The door was not locked when we came in."

"I left it undone as I was not sure you had your key with you," said Jason.

"Let's go. Where's the torch?"

Jason hesitated and then said, "In my room but the battery is nearly done."

"Don't worry, I have another one in my bedroom. Let's get it."

They left Lydia with Natasha and returned back down the corridor just as a faint light glowed from Jason's room. Terry gripped Jason's arm tightly and before Jason could do or say anything, Terry flung the door open and stopped dead. Sophia was standing in the middle of the room in a dressing gown holding the torch which was now flickering. Terry stared at her for a second, comprehension coming in a flash.

"We will talk about this later. Sophia, please, go to Natasha and see if you can help Lydia with her. Now," he said curtly.

Terry went to his room and produced another large flashlight, this time with a really strong beam. They went down the stairs and started to check all the rooms with Terry locking the front door first and then working from room to room. Terry stopped. "I'm a twit! Let's check the circuit breakers in the kitchen first. They may be off even if the electric is back on."

They went into the kitchen and Terry went over to a large box fixed to the side wall and opened the door revealing row upon row of switches. He grunted with satisfaction and flicked some of them. Suddenly they had light. "Excellent," he muttered. "Now we can see where we are going."

They checked all the rooms except the cellar as Terry knew the door was locked. Eventually, they went back up the stairs and carefully searched all the upstairs and drew a blank. Nothing! They then returned to Natasha's room. She was sitting up next to her mum with Sophia sitting at the end of the bed. She was still tearful but more lucid. Terry sat down next to her but his arm around her and gave her a gentle kiss. He looked at Lydia and shook his head.

"Come on, sweetie. Tell me, what happened?"

She looked at him and then a little haltingly started to explain.

"I went to bed after taking the pills and must have gone to sleep almost immediately as I don't remember anything until a noise woke me. It was really dark and I could hear the rain outside. I was still a bit woozy from the tablets. I cuddled back down into the duvet and had just closed my eyes again when something touched the duvet. I turned over and saw something standing next to me. Dad! I'm sorry! I freaked out. Jason, it wasn't you, was it? Or you, Dad? It was so dark I really couldn't see anything."

They both shook their heads. Natasha started to cry again.

"I didn't make it up! It wasn't a nightmare. Something or someone was in my room. I'm certain."

"Are you really sure, baby? I mean, some nightmares can seem very real. I know, I've had enough of them, believe me." Terry quizzed.

"Jason and I have searched the house and everything seems OK. I can't believe anybody could have got past us without us seeing them."

"Dad!"

"What is it, Jason?"

"On the floor."

"What?"

Terry looked down at where Jason was pointing. A tiny smear of fresh mud, still wet, was next to the bed.

Terry shifted his position to inspect it. He looked at Jason's bare feet and then at Lydia's boots and then at his own. "Not ours. And if not ours, then whose?" He looked around and scratched his head.

"I don't get it. Listen, Natasha. After you screamed, what happened? Anything you can remember?"

Natasha looked at her father for a long minute before answering. "I think there was a noise like the one that has woken me up before to start with. I'm not sure. Dad! I'm frightened."

"Of course, you are kitten. But it's fine. We are all here and you are safe. Nobody and nothing is ever going to hurt you while we are around. OK? Now, go down stairs with your mum and Sophia and have a strong cup of tea. Jason and I will be down in a minute."

"What's going on, Dad?" Jason asked looking worried as all the girls left. Terry looked grim.

"I don't know, Son, but as sure as little apples, I WILL find out! Let's search this room from top to bottom." Search as they could, they came up with nothing and except for the little mark on the floor.

"Something WAS here, that's for certain. Natasha was not making it up and that mud didn't arrive in a nightmare," said Terry. "Do you remember she took you to task for moving her things? Maybe someone has been in there before. How the hell would they have got in and perhaps, more to the point, how did they leave? She said that noises had kept her awake at night previously. I don't quite understand. Anyway, let's join them downstairs. Before we do that, would you like to explain what you got up to? No! Don't bother. I think it is quite plain, don't you?"

Jason shifted uncomfortably. "Sorry, Dad! We, er, Sophia and I, that is, well, we sort of got carried away and, er, fell asleep."

"Hmmm! Let's go downstairs. Natasha is more important than your little liaisons at this moment," said Terry, still looking very grim.

They joined the other in the kitchen. Natasha had regained her composure and with the others sat there, sipping her tea. Lydia got busy making some sandwiches for everyone. Jason sat next to Sophia with his arm around her. She looked very upset and close to tears as well. "I'm so sorry. I really am."

Lydia moved over to her and patted her arm. "It really is fine. Don't you start getting upset as well. We have all been there, haven't we, Terry?" she said rather pointingly.

Terry coughed and looked away.

They all sat there in silence. The rain had at last stopped. Not a sound could be heard. Suddenly, in the distance, a bang.

Then another and then closely followed by three more in quick succession. A pause, then another one. Terry jumped to his feet. “That was a gunshot, a shotgun if I’m not mistaken.”

Jason looked up. “That is probably old Harry Welford chasing his dogs.”

“Who the hell is Harry Welford?” said Terry, suddenly angry.

Jason went on to describe their meeting with Harry and the finding of the dead sheep. Terry and Jason went outside. The wind had died down as well and the moon was just beginning to show through the clouds. A long moaning cry echoed across the valley.

“Bloody hell! What the hell was that?” Terry exclaimed.

“I heard that same sound when Sophia and I were out on the cliffs just after I thought I had seen something moved in a cave out on the point,” Jason said.

“It’s enough to chill the blood,” muttered Terry. “I think I have heard that sound before. The other night! I thought I was imagining it. I thought something was watching the house and I went and checked it out. Someone had been in the garden by the trees. Bye the way, something you said earlier, Jason, about Harry finding this guy nearly dead out on the cliff path and then he coming here to phone and finding Dr Jackson here. Bit odd, wouldn’t you say?”

“Now you mention it, I suppose it was. Still, it was some 20 odd years ago.”

“Yes, I suppose it was,” said Terry unconvinced. He then told Jason about their visit to the Inn and meeting the three men and then about Davy. “You ought to have seen Dr Jackson and this guy Ho’s faces when I told them about the laboratory and even more so when I showed them the photo.

It was like they had seen a ghost. They tried to ignore as nothing but you know, I have had to interrogate some pretty tough cookies in my time and if they don't know something about it, I'll eat my hat. I'm sure one or the other was lying about the photo. I am going to get out my magnifying machine and have a good look at it in detail, especially the writing on the back. Also, tomorrow, I want you to take me to where you found that sheep and I would also like to have a talk with this chap, Harry. Is that OK with you?"

"Sure thing, Dad."

They went back indoors. Sophia was going to stay and sleep in the same room as Natasha but not in her actual bedroom, which she absolutely refused to do and no one could argue with that after her traumatic experience. They would use one of the other spare bedrooms. Terry had now locked Natasha's bedroom door after she had removed some extra clothes ready for the morning. After such an eventful day, they were all tired and went off to bed early.

* * * * *

Chapter Six
The Photo

It was still dark when Terry woke up. He lay there for a few seconds, wondering what had roused him. Lydia was still fast asleep, her blond hair peeping out from underneath the duvet. He was suddenly aware of a soft, regular tapping. He swung his legs out over the side of the bed and was standing up in one fluid movement, grabbing his shorts which he stepped into while moving rapidly to the door. The sound was coming from downstairs. Moving down the stairs lithely like a hunting cat, he realised somebody was outside tapping quietly on the door. He crept up to the door and slipped his fingers around the handle. His grip tightened on it and then violently ripped the door open. There was a short gasp and a man nearly fell inside. Terry recognised him immediately.

"Bloody hell, Davy, you made me jump. Do you know what time it is?"

"You said soon, Boss, so I came as soon as I could," Davy replied.

"Well, you had better come in and I'll get the kettle on and we'll have a brew while I bring you up to speed," said Terry.

"Good on you, Boss. I free wheeled the car down the drive as I didn't want to wake up the whole house."

They moved to the kitchen and over a cup of tea, Terry went over all that had happened.

"The thing is, I want to find out who the two guys are in the photo and what the connection is with the lab in the cellar," Terry explained. "Have a look while I get the magnifying machine out," and pulled out the scrap of photo for Davy to look at. They slid the paper under the glass and switched on the power. Terry played around with the focusing dials until the letters on the reverse side swam into view. The first four letters were, as Sophia had correctly identified, P>O>R>T.

Terry very slowly increased the magnification and using a different dial, which sharpened up the image. "Well, well! Look at that! O>N, if I am not mistaken." Terry moved the paper slightly to look beyond the faint letters. "D>O, is that a W? Yes, I think it is. And then another N." Terry looked at Davey in amazement. "Why didn't think of it before? Porton Down! Well, I'm dammed. Who would have thought of that?"

Davy looked a little perplexed. "What is so special about Porton Down?"

"Only this country's one and only and the largest germ and biological warfare laboratory centre in Europe."

"Oh, cripes!" Davey exclaimed. "What are you getting into, Boss?"

"I'm not sure, Davy, but I have to find out. There is something not right about all of this. I must make a phone call to a friend who I hope will be able to help. In the meanwhile, can you find some extension cable and some decent portable lights and anything else you can think of so we can get a good look at the cellar as I want you to have see what is down there."

"I'll get off then. It won't take me long to get that. Meet you back here in a couple of hours. OK, Boss?"

They both slipped out of the house and drove their respective cars up to the main road and then drove off in opposite directions as Terry knew there was a telephone box a mile or so up the road. In a short while, Terry had made the call and had returned to the house just in time to meet Lydia wandering around in the kitchen.

"I missed you, lover boy," she said, snuggling up to him and kissing his cheek. "Who was your friend?" Nodding to the two empty cups on the table.

"Davy. We deciphered the other letters on the photo. Porton Down! I have rung a friend who is going to help, I hope, to speak to someone in authority there, who may be able to help me find out who is in the photo."

"Davy was early, wasn't he?" commented Lydia.

"That's what I said to him but he pointed out I had said 'soon'. He is one of the best. Whatever he said about me, I was full of admiration for what he did for me on that last jolly. If it hadn't been for him, I wouldn't be here now. I was determined I was going to get him out of that hell hole if it was the last thing I did. It nearly was!"

Jason appeared downstairs with Natasha and Sophia close behind. Sophia was wearing some of Natasha's clothes as hers were still wet and covered in mud. "I should get off to work soon," she said.

Lydia made her drink a coffee and eat a slice of toast and then she made her goodbyes and kissed Jason firmly on the mouth. She then hurried out and roared off up the drive. Natasha still looked a bit shaky.

Davy was back within the promised two hours with a pile of equipment.

"Jason, can you give us a hand with this? Oh, by the way, this is Davy. He's a mate from way back."

Jason looked at Davy curiously.

"Hi! Davy. Dad, where do you want all this stuff?" Jason said.

"We will have to get it down to the cellar. We'll plug it in up here and unravel the cable down the steps. Just be very careful. The steps are very steep and it is a long way down," said Terry.

They carried all the equipment to the cellar doorway where Terry unlocked the door and together started on the long, dark descent, using the new torches Davy had brought, unravelling the electric cable from the reel which Davy was carrying. There was still quite a bad odour in the air. They then set up one of the flood lights at the bottom of the stairs to illuminate the passageway to the main doorway. Terry undid the massive bolts on this and with effort heaved the door open. Davy and Jason wrinkled up their noses as the heavy odour assailed them. It was definitely worse down here.

"Yah, Gods! Did something die down here or what?" Davy exclaimed.

"It's not good." Agreed Jason.

They set up the remaining two floodlights and switched them on. Immediately, the laboratory was shown up for what is was. Pools of light and deep shadows gave a surreal effect. Davey whistled in amazement. "This is really weird. I have never seen anything like it in my life before. This little set up must have cost a small fortune, Terry."

Terry looked at him quizzically. "You know, I hadn't even thought about that side of things but you are right. Somebody invested a lot of money in this and I mean, a lot! They also went to an awful amount of trouble to drag all this stuff down here. I mean, we were sweating just bringing all this cable and lights down."

Terry walked down between the benches and showed them where he had found the photo. Davy and Jason wandered around looking at all the equipment and especially at the broken mess of junk and glass on the floor.

"Terry," Davy called. "Have you noticed this?"

Terry walked over to them. "What is it?"

"Do you see this gap in the benches right here against the wall?" Davy asked, motioning with his hand in that direction. "Also, look at this armoured cable in the ceiling. It goes into the wall. Something must be in behind this."

Terry inspected it. "Hmm! I think you are right. How the hell can that be? Though, I mean the wall is made of solid granite blocks."

They all looked intently at it. Suddenly, Jason noticed something.

"If you stand back a bit, you can get a vague outline of a door way," he said. He walked back over to the wall again and ran his hands over it. "This stone sticks out a lot compared to all the others," he commented. "Look, the joints aren't filled in like the rest." He suddenly gave the stone a push. To all of their amazement, it slid away from him into a recess within the wall. There was rumble and then a grating, grinding noise and a whole section of the wall started to move. It took a full minute to open completely. The men all looked at each other. "Well I'll be blowed," said Terry. "Well done, Jason. That is amazing! I have heard of things like this but never thought I would ever see it for real. It is all about counter balancing and with the right amount of equal weight, even a small movement can move huge objects. The Egyptians were past masters at it."

Davy went over to the nearest floodlight, picked it up and carried it to the new opening and shone it in. They craned their heads to look inside. There was another large room, not quite so big as the first but still a decent size.

"Well, looky here!" he exclaimed. "I wonder who was kept in that?"

They looked curiously at a large cage, about ten feet square on one side of the room. It contained a large iron bed which was bolted to the floor with remains of some filthy bedding on it and what looked like a chemical toilet and a few various other items including a basin and a plastic water container beside it. There was another bed outside the cage further down the room. In the middle of the caged area, a large shackle had been cemented into the floor and attached to this is a long length of quite heavy chain with large manacle connected to the far end.

"They must have kept someone imprisoned down here. What a terrible place to have to live. But why? And who?" said Terry. "Look at the manacle. It's broken. And look at this. The chain is attached to a small winch outside the cage so that whoever was on the end of it could be dragged to one side away from the door. Maybe this explains the broken stuff next door. Maybe, whoever was kept here, broke out, had a fight with whoever and escaped."

"Maybe they didn't escape," said Davy thoughtfully. They all exchanged glances at that. "Maybe that would explain the large bolts on the outside door. Maybe whoever it was, was left down here but there is no sign of a body so that seems unlikely. Unless, of course, there is another way out of here."

"That is a hell of a lot of maybes," said Terry. "But I think you could be correct. Let's see if we can find another exit. It might be obscure like the entrance to this room."

They extended their area of search but without success. "If there is another exit, it must be well hidden," said Jason.

"Well, I think we are done here for the time. We need to fix the electrics down here so we can really see properly. Let's get back up," said Terry.

They retraced their steps back up the house where Terry carefully locked the main door to the cellar. They all trouped into the kitchen where the two girls were busy getting some food ready for them and brought them up to speed with what they had found. Davy had to leave to get back to the Inn to open up.

"Let me know if I can help you some more, Boss," said Davy.

"Actually, you can. Keep your ears and eyes open and try and find out all you can on our two friends. I just don't trust them."

Davy left and they heard him drive off.

"Come on, Jason, show me where this sheep was out on the cliffs," said Terry. The two of them went out and took the path down the valley towards the old mine workings and the engine house. They joined the main cliff path and after a while, Jason pointed ahead to a hedge in the distance.

"That's where Sophia fell over, by the stile into the bracken and put her hand on the dead sheep."

"Looks like someone is already there," said Terry.

"I think it's old Harry. Yes, I can see his camouflage jacket from here," said Jason. "What is he doing?"

They walked closer. Terry had a strange look on his face. "He's not moving. Quick, Jason, I think he's dead."

They raced up to the hedge. Harry was very dead. His body hung over the stile at an awkward angle. His shotgun lay on the ground in a large puddle of blood which had run down his arm apparently from a wound on his head which was curled under his arm. Terry very gently moved Harry's arm to expose his face. Jason gave a strangled, gurgled sound and turned to one side vomited a stream of mucus onto the grass. Terry winced at the sight. Harry only had one eye left. Where the other one should have been was now just a hole with a large chunk of his mouth and cheek missing exposing some yellow teeth now stained red with blood. The blood had congealed on the jacket in large gelatinous blobs mixed with lumps of flesh. A piece of his skull had been ripped off and part of brain was exposed. Altogether, a terrible sight. Terry let out a deep sigh and turned to Jason. "I'm sorry, Son, for you to have to see him like this. There is nothing we can do here to help him, poor chap. Jason, are you OK? You are not going to faint on me, are you?"

Jason looked at him, his face pale and he was trembling slightly. "I'm OK, Dad. What do you think happened to him?"

"At a rough guess, I would say he chased after those dogs you said he wanted to shoot, got to the stile, slipped, the shotgun went off in his face."

"But he struck me as being a very careful sort of guy and he obviously knew how to handle a gun."

"Maybe, but in the heat of the chase, perhaps he forgot to put the safety catch on. Now, don't touch anything. We will have to go and report this and get some help. Damn! This lack of mobile signals is a pain in the arse!"

Terry went right up to Harry's body and looked at it very closely.

"Jason, look at this! I think his other arm is broken and there is a large tear in his waterproof jacket all the way through to his camouflage coat. It's ripped to hell. How the hell could that have happened and especially if he was trying to fire his gun. I can't work out how he would have been able to do that if he had a broken arm. The arm must have been broken before he slipped on the stile. Maybe that is why he fell. All in all, rather peculiar."

"Dad!"

"Yes, Son."

"The sheep has gone!"

"What?"

"It's gone."

"Maybe Harry moved it?" Terry said in way of explanation.

"He said he was going to leave it as he said the dogs would back for another meal."

Terry took of his jacket and draped it over Harry's body as best he could. "Don't worry about the sheep. Let's just go and get some help. We will get back to the house, take the car to the telephone box and alert the authorities and then come back here to wait for them."

They walked briskly back along the cliff path, turned off by the old engine house and arrived back at the house. Jason went in to give the news of their sad find to the girls while Terry jumped into his car and roared off up the drive. A short while later, he was back.

"Jason, would you wait here and show them the way while I go back to Harry? I wouldn't want anyone accidently finding him as he is," Terry said grimly.

Some 25 minutes later, Jason re-joined his father at the style accompanied by two policemen and two paramedics carrying a folding stretcher. The police made a swift search of the area and photographed the whole scene with them taking particular care to record close ups of the body before they allowed the paramedics to put the stretcher nearby.

"We need to have a doctor to confirm details of death before we can move him," the Sergeant explained. "There is one coming."

Just then Terry spotted another figure hurrying towards them along the cliff path and he recognised him immediately.

"Dr Jackson! You got here quickly."

"The police contacted me and asked me to attend," the Doctor returned. He caught sight of Harry's body and was visibly shaken.

"Terrible! Terrible! What a waste of a lovely old man. I have told him endless times to take more care using that gun. Tragic! Obviously he hadn't put the safety catch on when he slipped. He never was very good on his feet. Getting too old for him to be charging around the cliffs at night," Dr Jackson muttered.

Terry and Jason exchanged glances but said nothing.

"Thank you for your help, Mr Knight, but we can handle things now," one of the policemen said. "Especially now that the Doctor's arrived."

Terry nodded. "I expect you will need a couple of statements in due course and you know where to find us when you are ready."

"Yes, Sir. Thank you."

Terry and Jason moved away down the path. Jason looked at his father. "How did the doctor know it happened at night? And what was that rubbish about him being a bit unstable on his feet? I don't think I have ever seen such a fit man for his age. When Sophia and I found his lost sheep, he came down the path here like a bloody mountain goat. Incidentally, I noticed you didn't mention the sheep to the police."

Terry just smiled but without mirth. "I think there is more to our good doctor than he would like us to know. Now show me where you thought you saw something in that cave."

They carried on walking until they arrived at the old mine shed. Jason pointed out across the sea to the point.

"Just over there, about 100 feet down from the top. You can just see a small opening."

Terry shielded his eyes from the reflection of the sea and squinted into the distance. "Hmm! Very difficult to access. That cliff is just about sheer."

"I may have imagined it, Dad. The weather was awful and with the storm…" Jason shrugged his shoulders.

"Maybe! Maybe not! Let's get back."

* * * * *

Chapter Seven
The Following Day

Terry looked at Lydia over breakfast and announced that he was going to drive to Salisbury to meet up with an old colleague.

Lydia looked surprised. "When did you arrange that?"

"Yesterday, after I had rung the police. Actually, not to meet my friend but to see someone he has managed for me to meet. It wasn't easy to get the appointment." Terry smiled broadly at her.

"Come on, let us in on the secret." Lydia smiled back.

"No less a person than the Director of Porton Down. I had to pull in some serious favours to be able to see him. Good job, I have a high security clearance even now."

"Dad, if it OK with you, can you drop me off in town as I am going to have to check in with the surf school and I would like to see Sophia at the same time," asked Jason.

"No problem, Son, but can you do me a favour? Ask around discretely, maybe Mrs Winston and Sophia. Also, try the police station. I am interested in knowing whether or not any other people, besides the ones we already know about, have gone missing in the last 40 years or so, especially in unusual or mysterious circumstances. It might be interesting.

You could make up some sort of story to explain your interest if you have to."

"No probs, Dad."

"So, let's go."

After dropping off Jason with his mind on all the currents events, Terry was not taking too much notice of the traffic and failed to see a car which was keeping pace with him which had pulled out a few cars behind him as he left the town behind and followed him at a respectful distance. If he had taken an interest in it, he would have seen two swarthy men, of eastern origin occupying the front seats.

Several hours later, after an uneventful drive, Terry turned off the main road to follow a sign which read 'H.M Porton Down Establishment M A F F'. He eventually came to another turning also signposted the same but in small print at the bottom 'Ministry of Defence'. The next sign read 'No Unauthorised Visitors. You May be Stopped for Security Checks'.

A little further on, he approached the entrance gates which were heavily guarded by several men in uniform. He noticed that behind them and inside the gates were some others which were standing around discretely and were carrying automatic weapons. A small but solidly built building, which appeared to be the guard house, was set slightly to one side of the heavy gates. High meshed fencing topped with razor wire ran away from the gate in both directions. Terry noticed an armed guard walking further along the fence with a very large Alsatian on a leash. A second fence as formidable as the first ran parallel to it several yards back. There were floodlights and cameras set on pillars as far the eye could see. A space had been set aside for visitor parking. He drew the car to a stop beside one of the officers who had raised his hand to him.

"Can we help you, sir?" he asked.

"Yes, I have an appointment with Doctor Faulkner," Terry pulled out his wallet and handed over his security card. "I'm Terry Knight."

The officer scrutinised the card, looked down at a clip board which he held in his hand and then handed the card back to Terry.

"Please, leave your car here, sir. If you would be kind enough to make your way to the main gate and my colleagues will check you in," he spoke quietly into a radio mike and then nodded to Terry. "This way, Major Knight, you are early but expected."

Terry was escorted to the gate, which at a nod from the guard accompanying him to his colleague the other side, slowly slid back and Terry walked through. He was guided to the blockhouse and once inside was patted down by one of the guards who then waved a type of wand over his body.

"He's clean, Sergeant."

"Thank you, Corporal." The Sergeant turned to Terry and said, "Your escort will be here in a moment, Major."

Just as he spoke, a land cruiser pulled up outside and Terry was escorted out to the car, a rear door was opened for him and he slid inside followed by another armed guard. The doors closed and the car set off. A few minutes later it pulled up outside what looked like a large office block. Two more armed guards stood outside the main entrance. His car door was opened by one of them.

"This way, Major, please, follow me."

He followed the new face into the building through the heavy glass doors and taken down a corridor to another doorway, which they passed through, into a room almost completely bare of any furniture and stopped in front of a thick opaque glassed partition with a touch screen console beside it. The guard stood back and motioned Terry forward.

"Please, be kind enough to place your hands flat on the screen," an unseen, metallic voice instructed. Terry complied. There was a series of blips and then the partition made a sudden hissing sound and slid open. A lady stood in front of Terry.

"Please, come in. Welcome to Porton Down, Major Knight. That was just to double check on your identity. Hand print analysis. Virtually impossible to fake. Dr Faulkner will be with you shortly. I am his secretary. May I get you a tea or a coffee?"

"A coffee would be good. Thank you."

"In the meantime, please, make yourself comfortable." She returned a few minutes later with two coffees, placing them on a small side table. "One for you and one for Dr Faulkner," she said smiling at his quizzical look. She then left the room through another doorway. The partition hissing shut behind her. Terry sat down and sipped at his drink.

Almost immediately, it hissed open again and an elderly, grey-haired man dressed immaculately in a dark blue suit entered the room. He approached Terry, his hand extended. His grip was unusually firm and Terry took an immediate liking to him.

"I am very pleased to meet you, Major Knight. I am Dr Faulkner and I am head of operations at Porton Down. You come highly recommended by Group and I have been instructed to answer as many of your questions as possible, providing you do not ask for details of what we do here. You are not cleared for that."

Terry looked surprised. "You are aware of Group and what it does?"

Dr Faulkner gave a little smile. "I, er! We have had dealings with Group before. Sometimes they are the only way things can get done. However, this is the first time I have ever met one of their team of special operatives. Our association was always conducted at, shall we say, at arm's length. I assume you are and not just SAS or SBS. So, what can I do for you?" he said in a very business-like tone.

Terry nodded. "Yes, you are correct. Sometimes, as you have already said, things need to be done off the record and even beyond the liberal parameters of the SAS. Even the PM was not privy to everything we did and our actions were sanctioned by Group headquarters only. I am now retired from all of that but in that line of work, you never really are allowed to give up and can be recalled at any time. I got injured for being too old and too slow, so I felt I should leave the younger and fitter guys get on with it." Terry paused and then continued, "I was wondering if you might be able to shed some light on this scrap of a photo I found in rather strange surroundings." Terry pulled the piece of paper from his pocket and handed it over.

Dr Faulkner put on his spectacles and peered at the photo.

"Why bring it to me?" he asked.

"Well, on the back someone has scribbled 'Porton Down' so this seemed as good a place to start as any," Terry replied.

“Ah! I see. Let me have a look.” He paused. The silence was total as he looked intensely at the photo. He raised his head and stared at Terry.

“Well, I never!” Dr Faulkner looked startled.

“You recognise the two men?”

The Doctor rubbed his chin and hesitated before answering as though he wasn’t sure whether or not to reply. He looked Terry in the eye and sighed slightly, nodded and then appeared to answer reluctantly.

“Yes, of course, I do. I took the picture.”

It was now Terry’s turn to look startled. “You did?”

“Yes. I worked with both of them a long time ago. We were all young then.”

“How long ago?” Terry asked.

“Oh, let me see. It must be about 40 odd years ago, I suppose. I had joined the team here around about then and these two guys were head hunted to assist me in the research. I was the team leader. We brought them over from America. They had been working on a parallel project for Dow Chemical Industries.”

Terry leaned forward in his chair. “Can you tell me the dctails?”

Dr Faulkner cleared his throat, reached for his coffee and slid into a large armchair. He took a sip and gave a little sigh. “I don’t see why not. It was a long time ago. What do you know about Agent Orange?”

“Who is he?”

“Wrong question, Major! Not who but what. Let me start at the beginning. A long time ago, during the Vietnam War, America was asked by South Vietnam to try and do something about the thick jungle which the Viet Cong were using to hide in and also used to ambush the allied forces, which they did very effectively.

"The Yanks looked into it and operation Ranch Hand was created. They used a flotilla of cargo planes specially equipped with tanks with a pump system and sprayer bars to fly low over the jungle in a staggered formation of usually four aircraft abreast, supported by helicopter gunships and recovery helicopters in the event of any of them getting shot down which very occasionally did happen. They kept this up very successfully as far as destroying the vegetation was concerned but as far as controlling the enemy, well, it had only a limited success. Unfortunately, the spraying was quite indiscriminate and a lot of innocent farmers and others got in the way with a horrible legacy for them to leave to their offspring.

"Agent Orange was the main herbicide used extensively by the Americans during the Vietnam War to de-foliate these jungles the Viet Cong hid in. It got its name from the colour of the drums it was stored in. There were other ones as well, Agent Blue and White but Orange was the principal and most dangerous one. Dow made the stuff. They used millions of gallons of the stuff which they sprayed over the jungle from the air and it was terribly effective but had awful side effects on the humans that got in the way and became contaminated with it. Well, over six million acres of jungle and farmland were totally destroyed. Unfortunately, during the manufacturing process, dioxins were produced, deadly ones to anything living with appalling results. At the time, they did not realise what their legacy would leave behind. It took time to work through but in humans it produced some really hideous mutations later in the children who were born from infected parents. This is apart from the hundreds of people, possibly thousands, who were killed by direct contact. I cannot stress enough the dangerous nature of these dioxins. They are probably the most lethal thing ever produced by man, especially as it occurred by accident. And I should know, bearing in mind the research we do here. You may have noticed the airlock on the door here. All rooms work on negative air pressure so that in the event of something escaping into the air from one of our experiments, air would come into the room when the door was opened and anything in it would not be able to get out into the atmosphere."

Terry shifted in his chair. "That is an amazing story! And a very worrying one." Both men were quiet for a while, immersed in their own thoughts.

Terry responded first. "I must say your security is very high and I am impressed but I am surprised. I thought your facilities would be a lot bigger."

The Doctor laughed out loud. "My dear Major, this is just the entrance and offices. All the research labs are well underground, which makes it an awful lot easier in the unlikely event of a leak. There is almost a small town down there and the passages run for miles. Some of the staff virtually live down there. We are completely self-contained. Anyway, to continue. Our team were given the task of trying to separate the dioxins from the herbicide without reducing the effectiveness of it. In addition to this, we were trying to see whether or not we could make humans immune to the dioxins and the effects they created. Not an easy task."

"What would have been the advantage of that?" Terry asked.

"It would have been huge. Can you imagine the advantages of an army that were virtually immune to biological warfare? You have been a soldier. You must know just how difficult it is to fight while dressed up in a bio suit."

Terry nodded in agreement. "It's not pleasant."

"Well, everything was going just fine for a while. Then we had problems. While my two colleagues were just about fanatical about our research, they went a step too far. Without any authorisation, they started testing on human tissue without my knowledge."

"But, surely, you must do that all the time," inquired Terry.

"Yes, we do, but not on LIVING human tissue. That was a major diversion of our brief for the research and definitely not allowed, not then and not now. I had the unpleasant task of reporting and then firing both of them as they refused to comply even after several warnings. Because of the nature of their work, we had to keep tabs on them for a few years."

"You mean surveillance?" Terry asked.

"Yes. One moved to the country and eventually the other moved abroad where we lost track of him. The Far East, if I remember correctly. Yes, that's right, I remember now, Korea."

"And who were they? I mean, their names?"

"The tall one was called Harvey Trelease and the other was Kevin Brent."

"Good God. Harvey Trelease! We are living in his old house. I think you should know that I have discovered a very large laboratory down in the cellars beneath the house packed with equipment."

Now it was the turn of the Doctor to look startled. He stared at Terry.

"That's not good news. Great heavens! What if that got out?"

"It could be even worse, Doctor. We found a secret room attached to it and it appeared that someone had been kept a prisoner down there as there was a cage with a bed in it."

The Doctor looked horrified. "Oh! My God! What if he had continued his work privately and maybe on humans? I said he was fanatical about his work but this was a long time ago."

"What would the incentive be for doing that? It would have cost a small fortune. Even the equipment I found down in the cellar must have cost far beyond my pay scale, let alone the cost of running an operation like that." Terry gasped.

"Major Knight, have you any idea at all on how much a foreign power would pay for this sort of research information? A kings' ransom! Believe me. Money would have been the least of his problems."

"Well, it's probably a good thing he is dead then," Terry commented.

"Yes, I know. I was told. A bad fall so the death certificate said."

"You are kept well informed, Doctor."

The Doctor inclined his head and gave a small smile. "I do like to keep up-to-date with events, even when it was 20 years ago."

Terry suddenly thought of something. "Who signed the death certificate?"

"Does it matter?"

"It could do."

"I can look it up quite easily. We always keep records of all our staff, alive, dead, past and present."

Dr Faulkner switched on a computer set on the small desk alongside him. Both of them were silent for a moment, the only sound was of the Doctor clicking the keys of his computer. He gave a small grunt of satisfaction.

"Are here we are. Yes. Let me see. There it is. A Dr Jackson. A GP from the local town."

"Jackson, eh! That man seems to get everywhere," Terry muttered.

"You know him?"

"Yes. A real strange one if I am any judge," Terry replied. "Incidentally, on what date did he die?"

"Oh! Let me see. Oh, yes. Date of death was recorded as being on 23 September, cause of death was violent contusion of the skull consistent with a fall from a height," said the Doctor, peering at the screen.

"What do we do now?" queried Terry.

Dr Faulkner rubbed his chin and thought for a minute. "I am not too sure except that I think we should send a bio team down to you so we can check out this laboratory and if necessary, make it safe."

"It will have to be done very discretely," said Terry.

"We are very good at being discrete." The Doctor smiled. "Is there anything else I can help you with?"

"No, thank you. You have been a great help. There were too many things going on which I couldn't understand."

"Expect a team down with you within 48 hours. Don't touch anything down there. Some of it could be highly toxic," said the Doctor. "Oh! Be extremely careful if you go anywhere near any liquids or find any gas containers."

Terry looked puzzled. “Why?”

“Well, if he had managed to achieve any sort of breakdown of the components, they could be highly inflammable and even explosive. After all, the original herbicide was concocted from derivatives of the petro-chemical industry.”

“Oh! Christ! It’s getting better and better.”

“Until we meet again, then. Good to know you, Major Knight.”

“Likewise, Doctor Faulkner,” said Terry, rising from his chair and shaking the Doctors’ hand. The Doctor gave Terry a very intense look and then the corners of his mouth twitched slightly and a small smile illuminated his face.

“I’ll see you out. The car will take you back to the main gate. Have a good trip back.”

Terry re-joined his car and drove back home deep in thought about the new revelations and again failed to notice the same car that had followed him earlier, slowly pulling out behind him as he left Porton Down.

Arriving home, he parked the car and entered the house.

“Hi, my darling,” Lydia whispered as she flung her arms around his neck and gave him a deep kiss. “Good trip?”

Terry sat down and then proceeded to tell the story to Lydia and Natasha. “So not very good news,” he said.

“Dad, would you unlock my bedroom door so I can get some more clothes?”

“Of course, honey. Let’s do it now.”

All three of them went upstairs and Terry unlocked the door and stood aside to let Natasha in. Natasha took a couple of steps and then screamed. Terry pushed past her and stopped in amazement.

The room was a shambles. Drawers had been pulled out, cupboard doors stood open, the contents strewn all over the floor.

"What is going on here? How the hell could this have happened and what's more? Who the hell did it and why? How did they get in?" Terry said angrily.

Natasha looked at her father. "Dad, the same way they came into my room while I was sleeping."

Terry looked at her and suddenly his eyes widened. "Of Course! You are right. There must be a secret entrance to this room similar to the one we found in the cellar."

He went around the room, examining everything as he went. After a while of poking and prodding the walls, he could find nothing out of the ordinary. He stood back scratching his head. He was puzzled.

How could this have happened? It then occurred to him that the only place he hadn't checked was the very large fireplace. He walked over to it and peered up into the huge chimney and gave a grunt of satisfaction. "I think I have found it. I just need to work out how it opens." His fingers suddenly touched a small stone which was much smoother than the rest. He gave it a push. Nothing! He then gripped it and twisted it. Somewhere deep inside the wall there was a muted rumble and very slowly part of the back of the fireplace started to move, exposing a dark tunnel behind as it gradually slid back.

"Dad, that is the sound, you know, the one I said I heard which woke me up." Natasha's face was very pale and she was clearly frightened.

"I think some of my clothes are missing but everything is in such a mess, I am not too sure exactly what."

Terry looked at her and Lydia slipped her arm around her waist to comfort her. Terry moved back into the fireplace and twisted the stone in the opposite direction. The back slowly closed with another low rumble. Terry looked up at Lydia. "I am going to get Davy from town so we can have a good look at this," he stated. "Lock the room again until I get back. I shouldn't be long."

* * * * *

Chapter Eight
Visitors

Davy was busy changing and connecting a fresh barrel to the bar lines. He finished the task and carefully closed the door and returned up the six steps back to the bar. As he entered, the outside door suddenly opened and two swarthy looking men walked in.

Davy turned to them and in a pleasant voice said, "Sorry, guys, but the pub not open yet."

One of the men stared at Davy while the other turned around and locked the door.

"Hey! What do you think you are doing? Unlock that door right now."

They ignored him and slowly walked up to the bar while still staring at him.

"Right, that's it! Get out, NOW."

One of the men lent his arm down on the bar top.

"We'll go when we are ready," he drawled. "We just want some information."

"I'm not telling you anything. Now just get out."

Just then, Davy's girlfriend, Di, having heard the raised voices, entered the room.

"What's the matter, Davy?"

Before she could move, one of the men grabbed her arm and swung her around facing Davy across the bar.

“Let go of me. You are hurting my arm.”

The man answered by twisting her arm up tightly behind her back until she let out a cry of pain.

Davy was getting angry. “Let go of her.”

“Not until you tell us what you know about Terry Knight,” the first man sneered in a heavily accented voice.

“I’m not telling you anything. Just get out and there won’t be any trouble.”

“You and who else?”

Davy had his hands below the counter and slowly lent forward.

“I don’t need anybody,” Davy said quietly. “You have just got me. Last chance!”

Without any warning, one of the men lashed out with his fist, catching Davy completely unawares. The blow caught him on the edge of his eye as he managed at the last minute to roll his head slightly to one side. A second slower and he would have caught the full force in the middle of his nose. Davy wiped his eye and then looked at the smear of blood on his hand where the force of the blow had broken the skin and looked hard at them. He slowly raised his other hand from below the bar.

The two men sniggered and then stopped dead, the smiles freezing on their faces. The snub-nosed automatic pistol, a Sig P320, which had almost magically appeared in Davy’s hand, pointed directly at the nearest man forehead, a crimson dot from the laser sights illuminating it.

“You want to play tough with me,” Davy said in a low voice. “Let’s see just how tough you are my friends. Now, I strongly suggest you let my little lady here go and leave while you still can. I will count to three and then if you are still here, you will really not like what will happen next. I shit you not!"

Very slowly, they backed away towards the doorway, releasing Di as they did so. Still facing Davy, one of them fumbled with the door lock before managing to unlock it.

"We will back to see you again," one of them growled, glaring at with Davy with hate filled eyes.

The door slammed behind them and there was a sound of a car revving loudly and then tyres spinning on the gravel.

Davy walked swiftly over to the door and relocked it before turning to Di and holding her tightly in his arms.

"It's OK, baby," he whispered. "Nobody is going to hurt. They have gone."

Tears ran down Di's cheek as she cuddled into Davy's chest.

"What if they come back as they said?" she exclaimed. "Would you really have shot them? What did they want? Why did they want to know about Mr Knight?"

Davy pushed Di slightly away from him so he could look directly into her eyes. "Questions, questions and more questions," he said smiling at her. "One, I think it very unlikely they will come back. I think they may have known that Terry and I have some history and they wanted to know how and why. As to why they would want that information, I just don't know. To disclose anything about Terry, well, that is never going to happen. To answer your other question, well, we will never really know, will we? I was expecting them to back down, which they did.

“They were not going to torture you and I not do anything. So, I guess, I would have, if it came to the push.” Davy’s expression hardened.

He gave her another cuddle and then a long kiss.

* * * * *

Chapter Nine
Exploring

Terry set off and drove directly to the Inn. He parked and swiftly jumped out and ran in through the door. Davy had his back to the door and was arranging glasses on the shelves and jumped around as Terry burst in.

"Blimey, Boss. You gave me a fright. What's on? You look worried."

Terry explained what had happen with the room and his visit to Porton Down.

"I'll give you all the details as we drive but I need you right now."

Terry stared at Davy. "What happened to your eye? That looks quite bad!"

"Oh! It's nothing to worry about. Just a small disagreement with a couple of guys who wanted to know everything I knew about you. I'll tell you later."

"What you tell them?"

"Nothing!"

"Good."

"OK, Boss. No problem. I'll just get my bag of goodies and let my girlfriend know she will have to man the fort until I can get back."

Davy disappeared out the back for a few minutes and then re-appeared carrying a large holdall which he placed carefully in the boot of the car.

"Just in case we need anything," he said with a cheeky grin. "OK, let's go, Boss."

On the drive back, Davy turned to Terry. "I was going to come and see you. You said to let you know if I found out anything. Well, earlier today, I had a visit from a couple of real bad dudes who were asking me about you and how I knew you from way back. The only people who knew that were the three guys you were talking to when you were here the other day."

"You say bad dudes?" Terry asked.

"Yeh! Real tough looking hombres. Looked Asian to me but spoke reasonably good English. They didn't like my answers either. Said they would be back."

"I can't imagine that would worry you. You are a pretty tough hombre yourself and I know you can handle yourself pretty well," commented Terry with a wry grin.

Davy returned the grin. "That makes two of us then Boss, doesn't it?"

"Just didn't duck in time," Davy said with a wry grin.

On the drive back to the house, Terry brought Davy up to speed with his meeting with Dr Faulkner and with what he had found in Natasha's bedroom.

"You've been busy, Boss. I am not surprised Natasha was frightened. Not nice. Someone somewhere isn't too happy with you being in the house. Have you thought about that? Plus those two dudes this morning. Too many things are rising to the surface, so watch your back if I am not there to watch it for you. OK?

"You are a good guy, Davy, and I feel a lot better having you around."

"Ere! Be careful, Boss. I could take that as a compliment!"

They soon arrived at Trelease House and when Terry stopped the car, Davy got out and went and lifted his bag out of the back, again, very carefully.

"Davy, what the hell have you got in there? You are carrying it around like it contains a rare collection of cut glass."

"Oh! Much better than that, Boss." Davy delved deep into the bag and pulled out two compact voice mikes and receivers. "These may come in handy."

"Good Lord! Where on earth did you get hold of those from? Actually, never mind. I don't think I want to know," said Terry grimly.

Davy just grinned. "Top of the range. Just like the rest of the stuff in here. No expense spared for the righteous." With that, he then pulled out a couple of Kevlar Jackets, follow that with two Glock semi-automatic pistols fitted with silencers and sighting lasers with a couple of spare magazines complete with shoulder holsters.

"Davy. I am amazed! I really think I ought to have a few words with your mother and the way she brought you up. Do you really think we may need this gear?"

Davy looked at Terry with a serious glance. "Boss, in my humble opinion, I think some serious shit went on down here and is still going on, especially after this morning's visitors. I don't aim to take any chances or let you do so either, so buckle up and let us find out what rocks. Just consider it as insurance with my compliments. Incidentally, my mother brought me up right and would have probably slapped both our backsides if she had known what you and I sometimes got up to."

Terry gave a grin and examined Davy's face for any form of humour.

There was none. He was deadly serious. They went inside and found the girls explaining what they were intending to do. Neither Lydia nor Natasha were too happy with this information.

"For goodness sake, guys! Is this really necessary? You might get hurt," said Lydia, obviously upset the way events were taking place.

Terry slipped his arm around her waist and kissed both of them. "I've been in a lot worse places but no one is going to invade my house and threaten or scare my family without some serious retribution," he said quietly. He looked at Davy who nodded his agreement. They went up to Natasha's bedroom. Davy gave a whistle through his teeth when he saw the mess. Terry went over to the fireplace and felt around until he found the smooth stone which he then twisted.

Again, there was a grating and low rumbling sound and very slowly the back of the fireplace slid to one side exposing a dark passageway.

They both put on the skull LED lights Davy had also brought and one by one slid into the space behind. They had barely squeezed through before without warning the fireplace started to close behind them.

"I expected that," said Terry. "Some sort of pressure plate set in the floor."

As soon as the wall closed, they were enveloped in total stygian darkness, so they clicked on their head light sets.

"Wait a minute, Davy. Switch your light off again."

Davy complied with Terry following suit. Terry gave a grunt of satisfaction. "OK! We can switch them on again. Look at this," Terry said. Davy peered at the point Terry was looking at. There was piece of rag stuck to the wall and as Terry moved it, a tiny pinprick of light shone through. Terry closed in on the light and put his eye against it.

"As I thought! A peep hole! Look through that and you can see right into the room without anyone in the room being aware that they are being spied on. Very clever! I couldn't work out how whoever was here would know when to access the secret door without being seen. Well, let us see where this leads, shall we?"

They turned and in single file walked down the passageway. At times the floor became quite uneven and they had to walk carefully with their heads down so the light from their headsets illuminated it. All the time the passage sloped downwards with some very sharp corners, sometimes to the left and some to the right. Steps going even further down, added to the problems. Suddenly, the passage divided. They looked at each other. "Left or right, Boss?"

"Your choice, Davy."

"To the right, then."

The tunnel was dank and water was starting to drip from the roof, making the floor slippery. The floor continued to slope downwards quite steeply.

Terry stopped and glanced at his watch. "We have been going for over half an hour now mostly downhill. We must be well below the house footings and probably below the cellar by now."

"Let's keep going, Boss. It has got to come out somewhere."

"OK!"

The tunnel abruptly split into three different directions. They took the right one again. After less than 50 yards, it split again into three.

They looked at each other. "We are going to get lost in this maze if we are nor careful. This place is like a rabbit warren. These tunnels must have been hacked out by the old miners but they knew where they were going," Terry said, rubbing his chin. "We should start to mark our way."

Davy rummaged about in his bag and pulled out a stick of chalk and held it up with a big grin. "Be prepared, my scout master always said."

"Davy, you are priceless!"

"Straight on Mc Duff." Davy scrawled the chalk stick on the centre passage wall with an arrow and they continued on into the darkness.

They slowly became aware of a sound of water splashing and shortly the tunnel widened out into a huge cavern. To one side, a channel had been cut in the floor and water poured down it in a fast-moving torrent. Water was also coming through the ceiling ever faster, making things very uncomfortable for them. Both of them were soaked through and starting to shiver in the cold.

"You didn't pack an umbrella in that bag of yours, did you? If so, this might be a really good time to get it out," said Terry with a wry grin.

"Sorry, Boss. The answer is no."

The cavern was vast, the ceiling in places so high that their head torches could not penetrate the darkness. The ground at this point had become very uneven with chunks of rock littering the floor, obviously having fallen from the roof but making their progress difficult and more than a bit dangerous. Neither of them would be in a good situation if either of them slipped and turned or even broke an ankle. They wended their way very carefully and slowly between the piles of rock. Terry stopped for a moment, turned and swung his head around, examining, as best he could, the walls of this enormous cavern. Suddenly, he paused and then slowly turned his head back.

There! He had not imagined it. Something has reflected the weak torchlight and shone brightly.

"Hang fire a minute, Davy. I want to have a look over here." Nodding in the direction of the light. They both slowly made their way over to the wall, the chips of rock rattling underfoot. The gleam came from within a deep recess in the wall. They shone their combined lights into the hole. Davy jumped back with a start. "Oh! My God! It's a skeleton," he muttered. Terry moved closer. "This has been here a long time. You can see that from what little is left of the clothes,"

Terry exclaimed. "I wonder who it could have been and who put it here."

Davy looked at him. "What do you mean?"

"Well, if you look carefully, you will see that the leg bones have been folded up under the rest of the body and the hands have been placed together. Also, it looks very much like this alcove has been hacked out much more recently than the rest of the tunnel almost as if it was done deliberately to protect the body from the water coming from above." Terry moved his light slowly across the bones. "Ha! Ha! Look at this. This is what reflected my light." He gently moved the skull to one side and retrieved a thin silver chain and unclipped the clasp. Attached was a small pendant, also of silver. It had a tiny inscription on the back. "Oh! Hell!" He breathed quietly. "So this is what happened to her."

"Sorry, Boss. I don't understand."

Terry held the pendant up so Davy could read it.

"Wendy, Love Mum. Always."

"Wendy! Who is Wendy?"

"Mrs Winston's daughter who disappeared 20 years ago while walking the cliffs after her dad died up on the path. I am pretty sure we have found her and this is her last resting place." They gazed at the remains, both subdued, their thoughts their own.

"Davy. Just look at this. What does this whole recess look like?"

Davy stared at it not comprehending.

"It's like a shrine. There are even the remains of some flowers either side of the body."

"Bloody hell! Boss. I think you are right. But why and by whom?"

"I don't know, man. Too many unanswered questions," Terry muttered. "Come on, let's move. We can try to sort this out later."

Somewhat reluctantly, they resumed their search to the far side of the cave. The cavern narrowed back to just a tunnel but this actually made things even more fraught with danger as the culvert beside the passage became a foaming torrent of water and the walkway became so narrow it became very tricky to walk along not helped by the fact that it was so slippery they nearly fell several times. The tunnel roof became lower, forcing them to crouch slightly as they scrambled along.

"Be careful of the roof, Boss, it doesn't look too stable to me."

Even as he said it, a thin trickle of stones cascaded on to the floor. The situation was not helped that Davy's headlight started to work spasmodically. He rounded a sharp corner a few steps ahead of Terry when his light went out completely. Suddenly, there was sound of a thump, a cry from Davy and then a loud splash. Another cry, this time muffled but despairing. "Boss."

Terry charged around the corner, his headlight illuminating the turbulent water just in time to spot Davy turning over and over in the current and rapidly disappearing into the darkness.

"Davy," Terry screamed after him but his cry went unanswered and he lost sight of him. A scuffling sound made him swing around, the dim light from his headlight not able to properly able to penetrate the stygian darkness. The tunnel had split yet again into three and for a split second he caught a glimpse of something, more like a shadow, moving away swiftly into the recess of one of the tunnels. Something large and indistinct in shape. His hand dropped to the butt of his automatic and with a speed born from years of hardened experience, drew the gun and fired off two rounds after it. The bullets whined of the walls of the tunnel but without any noticeable effect. Terry stood totally still but the only sound was the sound of the rushing water. He realised that he was very shocked by the sudden change of his situation and the recent discovery and he was now shivering violently from the cold and wet and the horrible realisation that Davy was gone, probably drowned in the fast running water. The bag of equipment had also gone down with Davy, who had strapped it across his back so his hands were free. He was alone! He must find a way to get back to the surface.

He selected a tunnel, not the one that the shadow had disappeared down and set off as fast as he could as much to help his circulation as for speed. After about ten minutes, he noticed that the tunnel had dried out and was now inclined upwards. This got steeper and steeper to the point that Terry had to crawl on his hands and knees. His trousers were ripped, his hands and knees cut and bleeding on the sharp spar like stones on the floor. He was covered in mud and slime as he slid and slivered, sometimes sliding back down the tunnel he had just crawled up as it was now so steep. Was it his imagination? No, it was not as dark as it was. He carefully reached up and flicked the headlight to the off position. Somewhere a little farther up ahead the darkness had paled and he realised he was nearing the surface. The tunnel was now almost vertical and barely wide enough for Terry to force his way upwards. He was forced to try and dig his toes into the sides to find any sort leverage. His thigh muscles burnt as though they were on fire. Suddenly, he felt something seize his ankle in a vice like grip. He started to slide backwards, dragged backwards, his ankle felt as if it was on fire with sharp points digging into it. He kicked down viciously with his other foot and felt it connect with something. The pressure on his leg eased slightly and he lashed out again, feeling contact. His ankle was released and he thrust himself upwards. He dug his toes into the sides again and groped frantically upwards pushing hard with his legs. Slowly, bit by bit, he was winning but he could hardly move, so tight was the tunnel. Stones and soil cascaded over his body and he had dust in his nostrils, eyes and ears but very slowly he was continuing to inch his way up. Eventually, he thrust a hand up and suddenly realised he had gripped a tuft of grass. He heaved himself upwards with a last supreme effort and the next minute his head had cleared the tunnel and he was breathing fresh air. He rolled over and lay on his back gasping for air. For all his fitness, he was exhausted. He realised then that the tunnel he had managed to crawl along must have been a ventilation shaft for the old mine and he was extremely lucky to have made it to the surface. He lay on his back, breathing heavily. Pulling his leg up, he inspected the ankle which had been gripped. In the light of the headlight, he was horrified to see the flesh was punctured with several deep wounds and was bleeding quite badly. What on earth could have caused that he wondered but did not have time to ponder. He was jerked out of his thoughts by a noise which chilled his blood. A low moaning sound, the same as he had heard the other night, reverberated across the valley. He listened intently. The thick damp mist obscured his view, more so because of the night. Moisture dripped of the bushes, soaking into his already wet clothes. A short pause. Then he heard it again, this time closer.

He struggled to his feet and took a couple of steps and nearly fell. One leg slid into the green slime. He managed to pull it out and stood again on firm ground. Switching on his head light, he looked around. There were tufts of grass and a few small hillocks from which some low bushes grew. The remainder of his view was obscured with reeds growing head high which rustled in the light breeze. With a sinking heart, he realised he had come up somewhere in the middle of the marsh and had absolutely no idea in which direction he should go. Furthermore, it appeared that something was coming in his direction. He could hear the undergrowth being forced aside a short distance away. His hand went to his gun holster but it was empty. The gun must have dropped out during his struggle up the shaft. Another groaning sound echoed across the valley, this time appreciably closer. Whatever it was, it appeared to be hunting him. A shiver went down his spine. It couldn't possibly see him, could it? But maybe it could smell him? An idea popped into his head and rolling over, he slid off the solid ground into the stinking slime of the marsh. He lay quietly with only the top of his head above the water having switched off his head light. He waited and kept very still, trying to regulate his breathing.

Some bushes rustled nearby and he heard the reeds beside him being slowly parted as something moved between them. Then something that sounded like a footstep squelched in the mud very close. He was aware of a large dark shape silhouetted by the slowly lightening sky as dawn approached. It was stationary for a moment and he heard a wheezing, sniffling sound and then this spine chilling moan which echoed once again, across the surrounding valley. It moved on and he lost sight of it. A few moments later, he heard the sound again but this time much further away. He realised he had been holding his breath and exhaled gratefully. Very carefully and slowly, he dragged himself out of the slush and back onto hard ground. What to do and which way to go was now his priority.

* * * * *

Chapter Ten
Other Developments

A telephone rang shrilly. The elderly man sitting at the desk picked up the handset.

"Yes! Oh! It's you. What has happened?" He listened intently for a moment or two. "So they followed him to Porton, did they? I hope they were not seen. No? Good." He listened again, getting more agitated. "None of this would have happened if you had dealt with it all those years ago. I did my bit and I am still waiting for the payday. By the time I get it at this rate, I will be too old to enjoy it. If he has had a chat to Faulkner, he will now know what it is all about. If I know Faulkner, he will be getting a bio team together to clear out the cellar as soon as possible. A pause. No, I think it unlikely he would have known who I was."

Another pause. "Yes, I agree. We must move the consignment immediately. This should have been done years ago. I am well aware that it needed time to, shall we say, ferment. What about our resident friend? Yes, I know. They were two good men but let's face it, we didn't expect that bloody thing to be still down there. It should have died 20 years ago. Then we lost the other two. After all, it had huge exposure to the Agent Orange derivatives that would have killed any normal creature. It would appear it had developed a certain amount of resistance to the dioxins.

"Maybe a clean sweep is needed? Give Faulkner and his friends a bit of a surprise. If we can get into the cellar, we could ensure they don't find out anything else."

The man was getting more agitated and angry.

"Yes, that is exactly what I mean. Those vats should go up with a very gratifying bang. After all, we no longer need all that stuff. We can access the tunnel from the mine house end, load it up and get the hell away from this place. Yes, the hoist is still there. You get some more muscle for loading and get Wan and Jo to get down to the cellar and lay up a surprise for our nosy friends."

The man coughed and then almost spat down the phone.

"I don't care if they are in the way. If they interfere, they will have to be put in the cellar and will go up with it. There is a very convenient cage down there." He sniggered at his own joke. "They can then come and help us guard the consignment. 8 o'clock tomorrow evening? Fine."

He put the phone down and drummed his fingers on the table. At last! Something definite, at last! After all these years of waiting!

* * * * *

Chapter Eleven
Rescue

Jason was worried and said as much to his mother. “Mum, they have been gone hours. Half the night, in fact. They must have had problems. Dad would have come back by now, otherwise as he would have known we would be concerned.”

“I think you might be right, Jason.” Dark circles now ringed Lydia’s eyes. “But what to do?”

Jason cocked his head to one side. “Listen. There is that bloody moaning call out there across the valley.” He paused. “I don’t really know.” Jason cocked his head again, listening. “Look, there it is again. I have had enough of this. I am going to see what this thing is.”

Lydia now looked really alarmed. “Oh! Jason. For goodness sake, be careful.”

“Don’t fret, Mum. I will. I’ll take Dad’s big torch, the new one and that old truncheon he keeps upstairs and I will be careful, I promise.” Jason ran upstairs and brought the items down and then shrugging on his waterproof, gave his mother a kiss and went outside.

The valley was partially obscured with a thick mist being blown in from the sea and a fine drizzly rain had started to fall. No moon was up and even had it been, probably would not have improved the visibility. Jason hesitated for a moment. Which way to go? Suddenly, from somewhere below him, in the depths of the valley, came a faint moaning cry. That confirmed the direction he was to take but even as he walked down the path, he remembered the warning Dr Jackson had given his father. Do not go out into the marsh especially at night. It is very dangerous. Well, that was exactly the direction he was taking. He shivered in the damp cold and pulled the collar of his anorak up higher. He stopped at a low hedge and peered down the hill towards the marsh. Only the sound of the reeds gently rustling the breeze disturbed the night. It had a slightly surreal feeling. He gripped the torch more tightly and checked the wooden truncheon was firmly stuck in his belt. What was that? He stared out into the night. Was he mistaken? No, there it was again. A faint glimmer of light which had appeared, disappeared and then re-appeared again. He had to start somewhere so that light position was as good as anything in the absence of any more sounds. He pulled out a tiny pocket compass and took a bearing on the light.

He set off down the slope until he reached the edge of the marsh. With the light from his torch, he thought he could see a faint track leading through the reeds. He carefully followed this trying to keep in the general direction of his compass bearing. The going became trickier with every footstep. Water squelched underfoot and he lost his footing a few times as he missed the firmer ground and slid into the morass. He could no longer see any light as the reeds grew up well above his head but he persevered. He was now sweating with the exertion. Moisture dripped of the reeds onto him making his progress very uncomfortable. Looking at his watch, he realised it had already taken him nearly 30 minutes to get this far. Swinging the torch around, he noticed the branches of a small tree which appeared to be growing on a low mound of dry ground. He thrust forward towards it and reaching, grabbed one of its branches and swung upwards. From his higher position, he could now see over the top of the reeds. Checking his compass bearing again, he peered through drizzle and mist. Yes, there it was again, not so far away this time. Climbing down, Jason set off in that direction, desperately trying to keep to harder ground. He fell heavily, cursing loudly and nearly lost his grip on the torch which swung around wildly. What was that? A sound? Pulling his feet out of the muddy slime he cursed again. No mistake. A shout! He shouted back.

"Jason?"

"Dad?"

"Yes."

Jason struggled towards the voice and pushing aside a clump of reeds, flashed the torch, illuminating Terry lying on a low bank.

"Oh! My God! At last! We have been so worried. Mum has been going out of her mind. How the hell did you get here?"

"Enough, Son! Help me up. I have hurt my ankle. Do you think you would be able to get us out of this godforsaken place and get back to the house?"

"I'll do my best, Dad. It is not going to be easy."

"Let's get home then. I'm just about done in."

Jason helped pull his father to his feet and with an arm around his waist to support him, turned and slipped and slithered back the way he had come, on a reciprocal compass bearing.

It took all of Jason's strength to help Terry, who was now limping quite badly. Several times, they took the wrong path and had to retreat back the way they had come. Eventually, they staggered out onto firmer ground with the marsh and its stinking mud behind them. They stopped for a few moments to get their breath back as they were both panting with the prolonged exertion.

Slowly, they made their way up the hill to the house with all its lights blazing which now stood a short distance away.

Lydia and Natasha were waiting for them and as they approached, ran down the path to them and with complete disregard to the filth and slime which now covered both the men, flung themselves at them, hugging them until Terry had to call a halt to it.

"Just get me to a shower so I can clean off all this shit," he growled.

They did just that but with a hundred unanswered questions.

"I'll tell all after I get cleaned up."

Lydia fussed around and after helping Terry to the bathroom, rushed downstairs again and put the kettle on to boil while Natasha made up some sandwiches. Jason went to his own shower and then dressed into some clean clothes.

A short time later, they were all together in the kitchen eating and warming themselves up with steaming mugs of tea.

Terry, sitting in his dressing gown, gave a slight grimace of pain. Lydia had dropped to her knees to look at his ankle with a first aid kit beside her. She inspected the deep puncture wounds and making sure they were clean, applied an antiseptic cream to them and then wound a bandage tightly round the ankle. She looked at him with a grim face.

"What on earth did this to you?"

"I wish I knew, my darling. I wish I knew!"

Terry then told them of all the events that had happened from the time he and Davy had entered the secret passage.

The others looked on, listening intently, horrified at the story.

"So you think Davy drowned?" Jason inquired.

"Must have," Terry muttered, obviously very upset.

They were all silent for a while with their own thoughts.

"Anyway, what if anything did you turn up at the police station on missing persons and unusual deaths?"

Jason looked at Terry. "Well, to start with, they thought I must be slightly crazy to be asking about things that happened maybe 40 years ago until I spoke to the sergeant there, who had been there a long time. He kindly went back into the records, as I had told him I was researching a book into the history of the town. What he found out was surprising even to him. Apparently, several! Apart from the ones we already know like Minny's husband and daughter, old Harry and Harvey Trelease, there were others." Jason looked around at his family.

"Well, go on, Son." Terry encouraged.

"Some 40 years ago, a young gipsy girl went missing from a camp on the outskirts of the town. Shortly after this, just a few days, a gypsy lad disappeared. Both the gipsy family and the police reckoned that in the absence of any other evidence, they had run off together and the search was called off. About a year later, another gypsy girl disappeared but after anther extensive search, nothing was found. But it is a bit suspicious that there were three missing in fairly quick succession. A few years later, a walker was found dead near the marsh. It was thought he had missed the path, fallen into the mud and unable to get out had then died before anyone found him. Then a bit of a gap until about 20 years ago. Then things start to get really interesting. The same time as Harvey Trelease was found dead, Minny's husband had his heart attack out on the cliffs on 23 September. Yes, that's right, Dad, the same day as Harvey Trelease died! Then a few months later, Wendy disappeared, never to be seen again until you discover her skeleton in the cavern. Sometime later, a few days apart, two bodies were washed up on beaches near here, badly mutilated, whether before they died or after was never clarified. They have never been identified except that they appeared to be foreign, possibly of eastern origin. A few years later, a similar event. Another two men, also badly mutilated Then, at various intervals, three other men with nothing to connect them found mysteriously dead on the moors. It would appear they were independent walkers and as they were found several years apart, no particular investigation was ever made. Hypothermia, a drowning and a fall were the reasons given for their deaths."

Jason looked around at his family.

"That is not the end of it! Fairly recently, in the last few years, no less than two other people have gone missing and two others were found dead at different times near the marsh but their deaths were put down as 'death by misadventure' and no investigation was taken into any of them."

"Why was that?" asked Terry

"Nobody seemed too sure why except that the deaths were confirmed by Dr Jackson. Apparently, he had classified some of them as death by natural causes. You know, heart attack, excessive exercise, etc, etc."

Jason looked around again. "The body count for a small town seems unusually high, don't you think?" he commented.

"Brilliant, Jason. Couldn't have done it better myself. I would take a small wager out with you that your sergeant was as surprised as we are."

"Yes. I don't think he could quite believe what he was telling me."

"Well, you just wait until I see him and tell him about Wendy's skeleton and Davy. I am not looking forward to having to tell Minny what I have found or for that matter. Davy's girlfriend," said Terry grimly. He groped into his dressing gown pocket and pulled out the little silver chain complete with its inscription for them to all see.

"So what do you think this is all about, Terry?" asked Lydia.

Terry gazed into the distance for a minute before answering. "I think Trelease was up to doing his research or whatever you would like to call it, after he was kicked out of Porton Down, possibly getting a human subject in the form of the gipsy girl who he probably thought would not be missed too much, in which, as it turned out, proved to be the case, then experimented on her with his cocktail of dioxins. Sometime later, the result of this, don't know how, turns into this monster which manages to escape killing Trelease in the process after a fight. This thing gets out into the old mine tunnels and somehow manages to survive, God knows how, up to and including now. I am absolutely positive this thing pushed Davy into the culvert and then later grabbed hold of my leg as I was trying to get out. Luckily for me, it didn't succeed. I am certain that had it done so, I would not be here now. What I can't quite work out is how this thing managed to get out and start to hunt me down so quickly after it had grabbed me. It certainly did not come up through the vent shaft that I escaped from or I would have seen it." Terry looked down at his heavily bandaged ankle. "I think this was done with its nails or claws or whatever it uses for hands. It is obviously very powerful just to have survived for so long. There are some bits to this, which still don't add up but I am now sure most of this is how it happened.

"But if this happened the way you say, Dad, how did it get into the mine and if there was a fight with Trelease, would it not have come up through the house?" Jason asked.

Terry looked at Jason and then smiled. "You know what, my boy, you are absolutely brilliant. Yes, I suspect it would have, had there been nobody else there but there was, wasn't there? Somebody else! What did old Harry say to you when he went for help? He possibly would not have known there was no phone, he just needed help. Somebody was here, our own mysterious Dr Jackson. I reckon he was here when all this kicked off and this would account for the bolted door down in the cellar. He managed to get Trelease out and then locked this thing down there so it couldn't get out probably hoping it would die down there. This was obviously not the case as it must have managed to access the old mine tunnels somehow from the cellar even though we could not find an entrance at the time we looked. It all begins to make sense now. But over such a long period of time." Terry pondered for a while and then looked up. "The bodies on the beach! That's it! After the dust had settled and they thought this thing would have been dead. They, whoever they are, sent some men down into the mine to recover what they had hidden in it. Assuming they had hidden something. It must have killed them. I am sure it would not have felt very affable to anyone who it may have thought had something to do with its imprisonment and possible torture. It has been there ever since. This is probably where the marsh and valley got its bad reputation from. Strange noises and vague sightings of things nobody could understand, people going missing, the odd unexplained dead body."

"That, then brings us to poor old Harry. It was not the dogs killing and chasing his sheep but this thing. After all, it would have had to eat and the sheep were very available," said Jason.

"I think you are right, Jason," Terry replied. "He waited for some dogs and found out too late it was something far more dangerous that he could ever have imagined. He must have got off a couple of rounds before the thing attacked him close up, they wrestled, his arm got broken, he managed to keep his finger on the trigger, fired off a few more rounds and then the gun was wrenched around, he either pulled the trigger himself or his finger was forced up, the gun fired and took half his head off. This thing then calmly picks up the dead sheep you found alongside the stile and walks off to its den in the mine to feast on it."

Everyone was quiet with their own thoughts. The family looked at him silently and shocked at his explanation.

Terry yawned. "I, we, must get a bit of sleep. I am totally bushed. We can't do anything until the morning anyway, then I will shoot off to the police and then on to the pub to see poor Di and Minny's to let them know what has happened."

Lydia went over to a drawer, opened it and pulled a small packet out. This done, she picked up a glass and half filled it with water.

"Pain killers for you, Mister Terry and no arguments even though I know you hate them!"

Terry gave a tired grin and held his hand out to take the glass.

"OK! Babe! No hassle."

With that, they all went to their rooms.

* * * * *

Chapter Twelve
Bad Things

Lydia woke up with a start and looked at Terry. He was still fast asleep, curled up in a foetal position next to her. No, she hadn't imagined it. The front door was being banged again, this time more insistently.

She slipped out of bed and grabbing her dressing gown, slipped it on over her nightie. As quietly as she could, she opened the bedroom door and crept out into the hallway, gently closing the door behind her. She did not know what time it was but it was getting light. She went down the stairs as the knocking started again.

"All right, all right, I'm coming," she called. Whoever it was must have heard her as the knocking stopped abruptly. Lydia slid back the door bolt and turned the handle to open it. As the catch cleared the lock, the door was so violently pushed open that she staggered back, recovered and before she could say anything, a large man pushed his way into the hallway with another just behind him. It wasn't so much the shock of this that startled Lydia, more the fact that the man had thrust a hand forward holding an automatic pistol which was now jammed rather painfully against her forehead.

"No sound or you are dead." He snarled at her. His colleague, who was carrying a holdall, which he placed on the floor, followed him into the hall, turned and carefully closed and locked the front door.

Leaving the first man covering Lydia, he went slowly from room to room, holding another automatic, which he pulled from his belt.

"All clear," he whispered as he completed his search of the rooms downstairs.

He fumbled in his bag and pulled out some cable ties and proceeded to fix them to Lydia's wrists. Then a roll of tape appeared and a strip applied to her mouth. With that done, the two men pulled her to the banister rail on the stairs and tied her to it with a piece of rope.

Satisfied that she could not move or call out, they slowly and quietly crept up the stairs. In a few minutes, they were back dragging a struggling Jason with them, similarly trussed and place him beside Lydia. They then ascended the stairs again. The first Terry knew was the barrel of a gun rammed into his ear while his arms were twisted together and the cable ties fixed to his wrists. The tape was placed around his mouth and then he was dragged unceremoniously out of bed and pushed roughly along the corridor. At the top of the stairs, he managed to turn and with his elbow, rammed it into the side of the man nearest to him causing him to stagger back with a loud grunt of pain. The man's partner reacted with considerable viciousness, slamming his gun barrel down onto the back of Terry's neck. Terry reeled down onto the floor at the top of the stairs. The man gave a nasty laugh and kicked Terry heavily in the ribs and then gave him a push which sent him rolling down the stairs. He tried to protect himself as he crashed down but only partially succeeded because of the cable ties holding his wrists, making it almost impossible for him save himself. He landed at the bottom with a thump which knocked the breath out of his body. As his vision cleared, the first thing he saw was Lydia and Jason trussed up like turkeys waiting to go into the oven. One of the men came down the stairs and attached a piece of rope to Terry and then fixed it to the other prisoners. In a short while, he was joined by his partner who in a much louder voice than previously said, "All clear upstairs as well." In a heavily accented voice.

Terry caught Lydia's and Jason's eye and slowly shook his head. Of Natasha, there was no sign.

Without any pause, with one man leading, yanking on the rope which was attached to all three of them, led them along the hallway towards the cellar door with the other man following on behind, pushing his gun into Terry's back to make him keep moving. Terry staggered slightly with the bruising he had received from being thrown down the stairs and also still limping from the injury to his ankle.

The door to the cellar was pulled open and then the whole party stopped. The man looked around and spotted the temporary light switch Terry had installed and switched them on. The stairs were suddenly bathed in harsh white light.

"My name is Wan and this is my friend, who is called Jo. Let me make this very clear to you. Any attempt to attack either of us or not complying with our instructions immediately will result in you being shot without warning. Do I make myself clear? Now you will descend down to the cellar. I will lead, you will follow and Jo will bring up the rear ready to shoot any of you who cause trouble for us."

The descent was difficult as they could not easily balance themselves with their arms tied in front of them. Several times, one or other of them stumbled and nearly fell, only to push into one another but eventually they arrived at the bottom in front of the large bolted door. Wan slid the bolts back and pulled the door open and waving his gun at them, motioned them to enter the laboratory part of the cellar. He looked around and hefting the holdall over one arm walked slowly over to the far wall. He gazed at it for a few moments and then as if making up his mind ran his hands over the wall. Pushing on the stone, there was a faint rumbling sound as the wall section slowly slid open. They all trouped through and Wan again motioned them towards the cage. When they were all in, he went over to each of them and ripped off the tape. He tore off Terry's last and gave him a big push, which made him step back. With that done, he attached the spare rope around their necks and tied it off to one of the bars of the cage.

"Oh, yes, I heard you were a big tough guy. I don't think you are so tough now, are you?" He sniggered. "Jo, go and do the business next door as he handed the holdall to him while I have some fun in here with our friends."

Jo nodded and disappeared back through the opening into the laboratory area.

Wan waved his gun under the noses of Jason and Terry. "You get over there where I can see you while I have some fun with this bit of blonde." With that, he untied Lydia and then seized a handful of her hair and forced her back against the old iron bed. "Quite a body on you, haven't you, babe?" He sneered. "Let's see what it all looks like, shall we?" he said coarsely and with that grabbed the front of her nightie and ripped it down exposing her white, still firm breasts. She gasped with shock and then started to realise what he was intending to do as he started to undo his belt and unzip the fly on his trousers. Terry started forward but stopped as Wan's gun waved in his direction. "Stay there." He snarled. "Or I will put a bullet in you just for fun."

Terry breathed hard, his face strained with suppressed effort. "You touch her, you bastard and I will personally choke the shit out of you." His hands were balled with fury, sweat dripping down his face, the rope around his neck straining into his flesh. Jason was watching as well, tears starting to well up in his eyes as he realised that they were both powerless to prevent what was obviously going to happen.

Wan just looked at him and grinned. "What you going to do, big boy?" And grinned again. He was a big man and obviously very strong and had no trouble holding Lydia with one hand.

Lydia was forced further and further back until she fell across the bed. Wan straddled her, holding his gun to her head. "Now, you just be nice to me and I won't hurt you too much." He giggled as he pinned her down. She tried to hit him but he smothered her attempt easily. Suddenly, she twisted her body and with all her strength brought her knee up, catching Wan in the crutch. He gave a grunt of pain and without a second of delay smashed his hand across her face. Blood spurted from her nose and ran down her face.

"You are going to wish you hadn't done that." He leered and with that he pushed his trousers down to his ankles and forced himself between her legs.

Lydia, now lying completely stretched out under his bulk, scrabbled with her tied hands on the floor for anything she could use as a weapon. Her fingers frantically searching. What was that? Something around. She relaxed her body for a second and Wan laughed. “Given up, have you, baby?”

She slipped her fingers around the object and suddenly realised what she had hold of. Something with a very sharp point. Wan went to tear her clothing down even further and then lunged towards her. Her hands holding what she knew now was a hypodermic syringe, rammed the pointed end into his naked side, her palm pushing the plunger in as far as it would go at the same time.

Wan let off a scream of pain and rising up above her slammed his fist into her chin. Her head jerked back with the force and more blood poured out of a badly cut lip. For a few seconds, she could not focus her eyes. She was aware that he had slid off her and was now kneeling in front of her. His trousers still down around his ankles but he seemed to be have something wrong with him. His automatic pistol dropped from his nerveless fingers. He was jerking spasmodically and as her eyes now started to see him again, his face was contorting in strange ways. He didn’t seem to be able to speak, although his mouth was opening and closing and as she watched, the pupils in his eyes seemed to disappear into the back of his head. His head shook and then he turned and vomited violently onto the floor. Mucus and snot started to pour from his nostrils. His condition worsened rapidly and he rolled over on the floor, twisting and turning. Blood started to ooze from ears and nose and his eyes were turning bright red and bulged out from his face, leaking a sort of puss and matter from them. Suddenly, they burst in a mass of blood and jelly which dripped down his cheeks. He was incapable of sound and just writhed around in front of a terrified Lydia. Totally horrified, she could only watch as to compound the sight, Wan's skin started to blotch, first with bright red marks and then bubbling into large lesions which suppurated with even more puss.

Terry and Jason looked on unable to do anything.

Wan wriggled and writhed for a few moments longer and then with a strangled gurgle rolled over onto his back and lay still.

There was complete silence which was broken only when Terry, in a loud whisper, called to Lydia, who sat on the bed in a complete state of shock, staring at the inert form at her feet.

"Lydia, my love, come over here and try to untie me," he said gently. She was beyond his voice, so traumatised as she was.

"Jason, we have to get free before Jo gets back from the other room but I can hardly move. Can you?"

Jason just stared at his mother and the body as well and seemed incapable of any sort of reaction.

The moment for action was now lost as just at that moment Jo came back into the room and taking in the situation at a glance, drew his gun from its holster, pointing it first at one and then another of them. He went over to Wan's body and prodded it with his foot. He waved his gun over them but could not work out what had happened. He approached Terry and without warning slashed the barrel viciously across his face cutting the skin from which blood started to pulse out from.

"What the fuck is going on here? I am going to shoot you all, you motherfuckers," he screamed. It then slowly dawned on him that neither Terry nor Jason could possibly have been responsible for his partner's condition as they were still trussed up like chickens. He stood back, now unsure of what he should do next. He looked down at Lydia who was still staring fixedly at Wan's body.

"It must be you, you bitch, so you are going to get it first." And slowly raised his gun in line with her head. She seemed totally oblivious to what he intended to do.

Terry couldn't believe this was happening and was incapable of doing anything to intervene. All of a sudden his attention was drawn to an old dusty mat lying on the floor. It was moving very slowly, actually rising up in the air, being pushed up by a section of floor which was opening up under it.

Jo brought up his gun and pushed it against Lydia's head. "Bitch," he screamed again at her. He extended his arm but his attention was suddenly switched to the very slight rumbling sound emanating from the floor behind him. He swung around with a look of total surprise in his eyes, gun waving wildly. Terry was now aware of a very small red spot which had suddenly appeared in the middle of Jo's head. Terry closed his eyes. He could no longer watch the murder of his lovely wife. A feeling of total helplessness enveloped him as he waited for the shot. What he heard was something that sounded like a loud cough. His eyes flashed open in time to see Jo teetering to one side with a hole that had appeared between his eyes. Jo collapsed in a heap in front of Lydia not to move again.

His gaze went back to the ever widening hole under the mat. A hand slid over the edge of the opening followed by a tousled head of hair and then with a flourish, the rest of the body emerged from the hole. An automatic fitted with a laser sight was clutched in his hand.

Terry's eyes widened in amazement, which turned immediately to a feeling of total joy.

"Davy! In the nick of time! How the hell…I mean, what the devil happened. I mean, I don't care but, oh! My God."

"Hi, Boss. Just passing, you know. Glad to be of help if you know what I mean."

"Get over here now and get us out of these cables and ropes."

Davy walked a little unsteadily over to the two men and pulling a small but very sharp pocket knife out of his trousers, sliced through the rope and then the cable ties which were binding them. Terry and Jason rushed over to Lydia and freed her hands, Terry sliding his arms around her waist as he sat down beside her. She continued to stare at the bodies at her feet for a few moments and then the spell broke and she crushed her face into Terry's neck and sobbed. Her tears dripped down her cheeks.

"There, there, it is OK now, my darling. You are safe. You were wonderful."

Terry looked up at the two other men lying spread-eagled on the floor. "What the hell was in that syringe? I have never seen anything like it and I am pretty sure I don't want to ever again. Like some sort of nerve agent but much worse and more rapid."

They both shook their heads. Terry looked at Davy. "I thought you were dead, drowned. What happened? How did you get out? What hit you?"

Davy smiled at Terry wearily. He was obviously exhausted and filthy dirty. "Questions, questions, Boss, always questions." He gave a grin.

"I just didn't see what hit me except that whatever it was packed a wallop. I hit the water like a bag of spuds but luckily, I had my holdall handles over my back so I went in with it and managed to keep hold of it. I got washed down quite a way, it seemed like ages but, eventually, the current eased and then I must have bumped into a ledge or something which I managed to hang onto. Bit by bit, I managed to drag myself out onto the rock. It was bloody freezing, I don't mind telling you. I then managed to get my light working again, although it did go out again from time to time. I have been trailing around down ever since. The bloody place is like a rabbit warren but I still had my bit of chalk and if I came to a dead end, I just retraced back to where I had left my last mark and took a different passage. I heard some moaning sounds occasionally but they always seemed a long way off. I tell you, Boss, there is something real nasty down there, you know? There is a set of railway lines like narrow gauge, which I assume was used to move ore down in some of the passages. I thought that if I followed a set which slopped upwards, I might just find my way to the surface or at least near it. I then found some evidence that the passage I was in had been used as a sort of a store, so I just followed the tracks until I found the steps which ran up to this cellar. The lines come right to the bottom of the steps. It seemed I got here just in time."

"Davy, you are a fucking marvel! We must get us all out of here. Lydia and Jason are in shock. It has been a real bad situation for them and apart from that, you look as if you could do with a bit of R&R."

"Boss, you don't look to healthy to me either and I think your face could do with a few stitches. They worked you over pretty good, I think."

Terry lifted Lydia up off the bed, pulling her ripped gown around her. She was still trembling. "Natasha," she cried out.

Terry looked at her for a second. "Oh! Christ! I nearly forgot. How could I do that! These two heavies surprised us and searched the house but didn't find her. I don't know where she could be. Maybe she heard what was going down and went and hid but these two thugs were very professional and I think they would have found her if she was there which begs the question, where the hell is she?"

"Boss! Let's get upstairs and have a proper search for her."

"Those thugs were going to kill all of us. That is without doubt as they made no attempt to cover their faces and they even told us their names, so in a way it was just as well Natasha wasn't here because if you hadn't turned up, we would be all dead by now," stated Terry.

Terry, supporting Lydia and with Davy and Jason following went through the door into the laboratory area and started to make their way across to the other door.

Suddenly, Terry stopped, so abruptly that Davy, who was following bumped into him.

Terry put a hand wearily to his head. "I'm not thinking straight," he muttered. He turned and looked at Davy.

"What was that Jo up to in here while his mate was trying to entertain us? He was in here for quite a long time."

Davy looked at him suspiciously. "We had better do a check, Boss, before we do anything else. Maybe Jason can get your missus upstairs while we look."

Lydia appeared to recover slightly, turned to Terry and although still trembling, shook her head violently. "Please, don't leave me. I'll stay with Jason but I'm not going to leave you down here and that is final."

Terry gave her a hard look and rapidly came to a decision. "OK, sweetheart, you just sit here on one of these tables with Jason and I'll go and have a search with Davy. I'll be as quick as I can, I promise."

He followed Davy, who was slowly checking the rows of tables, both on top and below them. Terry chose a different row and started to do the same. They thoroughly searched up and down the rows without finding anything. Davy stroked his chin thoughtfully and looking around, said, "Well, that only leaves the vats at the far end, so let's have a look there, shall we, Boss?"

They walked towards them when suddenly Davy stretched out a hand and gripped Terry's arm fiercely. "Stop! Don't move, Boss!"

"What's the matter?"

Davy pointed to the floor. "That's the matter, Boss!"

A tiny, thin strand of wire was stretched tightly just a few inches above the floor with one end tied to one of the legs of a table. One more step and they would have blundered into it.

"Trip wire," said Davy. "I nearly missed it. Just saw a glitter of metal. Must be getting old and careless," he said with a rueful grin.

"So that is what he was up to," muttered Terry.

"Let's find out where the other end on this wire goes, shall we?"

Davy very carefully stepped over the wire, Terry following. They slowly followed the strand across the floor to the vats against the wall. Davy bent down to look underneath.

"Oh! Oh! Not good, Boss. Look at this. Real professional job if I may be so bold."

He pointed to a small box fixed to the bottom of the vat. Another wire ran tightly from it to the next vat and then again on to the third one. Davy moving with extreme care investigated the second vat and then the third one. He stopped and looked up at Terry.

"We have a problem, Boss. This is no kitchen sink bomb. This is a real proper job one, er, actually three. There is another trip wire over on the other side as well, so that whichever direction you approached this, you were very likely to set this all off." He bent down to inspect one of the devices more closely.

"They appear to have a timer on each of them and if I am not 'Bomber' Bates, also a trembler trigger which makes life very tricky.

"Our friend Jo did not intend anyone to mess with these." He looked up at Terry. "From what you told me about the potential of what could be in these vats, these things could make a very nasty hole in your house. So, for once, I'm giving you the orders, Boss. Get back to Jason and your missus and get the hell out of the house. Now!"

Terry stared at Davy and then at the bombs. "I can't leave you down here alone," he said aghast.

"Look, Major, sir! This is what I was trained for and I am very good at it. If I can't deal with this, then it all goes up bang. No point in both of us getting killed, is there? So just be a good little officer and let me get on with it. You KNOW…I had to deal with some real bad arsed IED's in the past, so get the hell away from here. I'm not sure how much time I have until I have a closer look at the timers. Now, just go!"

Terry face had clouded over and he looked grim. He nodded his acceptance to Davy and with a sigh held out his hand which Davy grasped firmly. "You're one of the best, Davy. Be careful." Then laughed. "I sure I don't need to tell you that."

"Piss off and get your family to safety."

Terry turned and stepping over the trip wire again, retraced his steps back to where Lydia and Jason still sat. Putting his arm around her waist, he gently lifted her down.

"We got go and find Natasha and get out of here as quick as we can."

"What about Davy, Dad?" Jason asked.

Terry's eyes watered with emotion. "We have got to leave him here to deal with the bombs our friend Jo left. Davy is very good at what he does, so we have got to put our trust in him. He wasn't nicknamed 'Bomber' for nothing. He saved me more times than I care to think about but we must move NOW, so let's go."

They made their way to the heavy entrance door leading to the stairs and as quickly as possible staggered their way up to the top. They were all panting with the exertion as they exited the cellar into the hall. Terry was so intent on helping Lydia who was leaning heavily against him. He didn't notice anything amiss until Jason let out a gasp of surprise. Standing directly in front of them were three figures dressed in biological warfare suits. The front door was open but was hanging at a crazy angle attached to the wall by only one hinge. Two of the men standing slightly behind the third were holding heavy automatic weapons. The leading man held up his hand to halt his colleagues and stepping forward and in a slightly muffled voice said, “Sorry, but it appears we are a bit late, Major Terry.”

Terry stared at the man for a few seconds before recognition dawned on him.

“Dr Faulkner?”

“The very same,” he answered, his voice muffled by the hood. “You all look beat and I think maybe you could do with a few stitches in your face.” He then raised a hand to his neck and unzipped the hood enclosing his respirator and lifted it off his shoulders.

“You have to leave, Doctor.” Terry grated abruptly. “There are three bombs in the cellar attached to the vats I told you about and Davy is trying right now to de-fuse them and I don’t know if we have much time left.”

The Doctor stared at him for a nano-second and then snapped his hand at the men behind him. One rushed forward to help take Lydia’s arm while the other helped Terry who was wobbling unsteadily. They all exited the front door and to the amazement of Terry and the others, found several vehicles parked up outside together with another group of men busily putting on their bio suits which they were removing from a large truck. Some more men were standing beyond them in a semi-circle covering the drive holding automatic weapons. Dr Faulkner gestured to another two men who were standing wearing paramedic uniforms beside a strange looking truck. They ran up and took charge of Terry, leading him up into the back of the truck. The rear door hissed open as one of them punched a button.

"Don't worry, Major, they will get you cleaned and stitched up and give your family the once over as well. This is a special detox wagon and medic centre. Relax! You are in safe hands. We will try to give Davy any help he may need."

"Natasha! I must find Natasha. She was in the house but we can't find her. I must look for her and get her out of the house," Terry shouted, now very alarmed.

Faulkner turned to him and said, "Major, if she is here, we will find her, please, trust me. Now be a good chap and let my men clean you up. You are no good to anyone in your current condition."

He gestured to his two companions to follow him and re-adjusted his bio suit hood, zipped it up and then ran down the corridor to the cellar door at a speed which belied his years.

* * * * *

Chapter Thirteen
Natasha

Natasha had indeed been in her bedroom in the house but ever since the incursion by something unknown, she still had problems sleeping and had only dozed fitfully through the night for a few hours at a time.

So, when the knocking had started on the front door, it had roused her. She rolled over onto her back, not properly awake, staring at the ceiling as light was just starting to creep through the curtains, wondering if she should go and see who would be calling at this time in the morning. Straining her ears, she thought she heard her parent's door catch open, so she relaxed and closed her eyes again.

Suddenly, her eyes flashed open. What was that? A muffled commotion along the hallway and she thought she heard a grunt of pain. She slipped out of bed and quietly opened her door and peeped out. With a growing sense of horror, she saw her dad lying on the floor near the stairs and then the two men laughing as one of them giving him kick which sent him crashing down the stairs and out of sight and them laughing to each other as they watched him fall.

She closed the door as quietly as she could and stood there for a second wondering what to do. If she stayed where she was, there was no doubt she would be discovered but as she looked around her bedroom, she realised that she had no weapon capable of dealing with the intruders so maybe she could hide. The problem was where? She looked around again but everywhere seemed too obvious but then she had a flash of inspiration. The fireplace secret passage! She quickly went over to the hidden stone and pushed it the same as her dad had done. It slid into the recess and a very low rumbling sound emanated from the stone wall and very slowly the gap opened. No time to lose. She could hear someone coming along the hallway. She squeezed into the passageway behind and just as soon as she entered, the doorway reversed and slowly closed. She felt around in the darkness, found and moved the rag covering the peep hole her dad had told her about, so she could look into her bedroom. Hardly had she done this when her door quietly opened and a man came into view. He stood still for a moment and then went round the room opening cupboard doors, pushing clothes in her wardrobe to one side to check and then even looked under the bed. He stood in the centre of the room looking around, then shrugging his shoulders, disappeared out of sight through the door.

Natasha stood rigidly still for a few seconds and then started to shiver violently as reaction to her narrow escape from capture started to sink in.

She groped around in the total darkness for anything that resembled a trigger to open the secret door so she could get back into her bedroom. After quite a while, she started to realise that she could not find it, try as she might. Tears started to trickle down her cheeks as the seriousness of her situation dawned on her. Incarcerated in a pitch-black tunnel while her family were being assaulted by armed men and unable to raise the alarm or even be able to get back into her bedroom.

Natasha started to move down the tunnel, using her hands to guide herself by touching the walls on either side. Her progress was painfully slow and she stumbled several times on the uneven floor.

Her thoughts raced and all she could think of was that she needed to rescue her family. How was something she had absolutely no idea of even where to start but first things first! She had to concentrate on how she was going to get out of her current predicament.

* * * * *

Chapter Fourteen
Close Call

Sweat dripped down Davy's face. He ran the back of his hand across his forehead and wiped the moisture out of his eyes as he squinted at the small box tied against the pipe leading to the largest vat. The trip wires had been the easy bit to remove from the bombs and they lay harmlessly on the floor where he had discarded them.

All three were connected together but the main box in front of him was the trigger for the other two. The timer had a small digital display which was slowly counting down. Three minutes left. No pressure then. Only the trembler to disable. Only!

He eased the tiny cover away from the box very, very carefully, uncovering a minuscule needle which swung very slightly from side to side. Very gently and with infinite patience, he picked up the matchstick he had already prepared, from between his lips and placing it between his thumb and forefinger, slowly moved it into position under the needle.

His hand trembled ever so slightly and he paused. One minute thirty-three seconds. The digital readout glared out the figures. He wiped his face again and blinked rapidly. He took a deep breath and held it.

He moved the tip of the matchstick to intercept the wavering needle. Immediately, it jammed the needle against side of the box, away from the metal terminal. He exhaled noisily. So far so good!

50 seconds to go. Out of his side pocket, he pulled a small but very sharp set of wire snips, manoeuvring it extremely carefully, positioning it against the main cable. His fingers tightened around the handles.

Suddenly, a noise behind him made him swivel his gaze. A man in a bio suit stood a few yards away from him. "You must leave now," he shouted at Davy.

Davy's fingers clamped down. The sharp snips sliced into the wires. "Too late," he muttered. The digital countdown had stopped. Perspiration dripped onto the floor in front of him as his head touched it. 15 seconds from disaster. A gloved hand clamped onto his shoulder. "Are you all right, sir?" said a voice, which seemed to be coming from a long way away. Davy slowly got to his feet and bending down, grasped the box firmly in his hand, ripping it away from the tape which had bound it to the pipe and tucked it into his pocket. He looked up at the hooded figure.

"I am now."

He swayed slightly and would have fallen, had it not been for the man's arm which he had put around Davy's waist. "Come on, sir, let me help you upstairs."

Davy was suddenly very tired and allowed himself to be guided to the doorway and eventually up the steps to the hallway. Two men were there in deep discussion which they broke off as they appeared. The older man looked down at the box sticking out of Davy's pocket. A wide smile illuminated his face.

"You must be 'Bomber Bates'. I have heard a bit about you one way or another. Your reputation was obviously well-founded. Absolutely brilliant, young man, if you don't mind me saying so. I am Dr Faulkner. Your friends are being well-cared for by the paramedics outside where I think you should go and join them as you look exhausted. Oh! Quick, catch him!"

Davy's eyes slowly turned up and his knees gave way and he would have fallen to the floor, had the man standing behind him not grabbed him.

The Doctor turned to his colleagues. "Take him to one of the bedrooms and get the medics up to sort him out while we get on in the cellars and try to clean this mess up," he ordered.

* * * * *

Chapter Fifteen
Revelations

Of Natasha, there was no sign of where she was or could have been. Dr Faulkner and his men searched the house from top to bottom without success. The remainder of the Knight family after their wounds had been cleaned, treated and where possible bandaged of the accompanying paramedics attached to the doctor's party were ordered to their beds to rest.

Terry had come off the worst, having to have six stitches put in his cheek where he had been slashed with the gun barrel from just below his eye to his chin. They had also re-bandaged his ankle. He had two suspected cracked ribs which they thought he had received when he was kicked down the stairs.

Lydia's face was swelling up with livid bruises with one of her eyes already nearly closed and turning purple. Luckily, her nose had not been broken but was naturally enough, very sore. It was obvious she was very traumatised with the recent events. Jason appeared to have been the least affected and jumped up out of his chair to help his parents up the stairs to the bedroom. They had already been given some pain killers and some sedatives to help them sleep.

Davy, the hero of the day, had taken a hot shower and gone straight to bed absolutely exhausted. He arranged with the Doctor to have a message sent to Di so she would know he was OK and would see her just as soon as he could.

Two armed guards wearing full balaclava face masks were left to look after their safety, one patrolling the upstairs landing with the other standing guard at the bottom of the stairs while the remainder of the doctor's team went to work in the cellars, clearing out as much as they could to make the whole area safe. Computers were unplugged from their stations, brought up the stairs and loaded into one of several large trucks parked outside. As soon as one had been filled, it set off up the road with an armed escort following in a black Range Rover. Much more difficult to deal with were the large vats at the far end of the laboratory. That their contents were of a volatile nature was in no doubt as this was where the explosives had been placed and this would not have been done without prior knowledge of the contents as yet unidentified.

The technicians under the Doctor's orders eventually ordered everyone else out of the cellar, the main items having been now cleared out. Working slowly and very carefully with their bio suits fully sealed, they ran a number of flexible pipes from a strange looking tanker parked outside down into the cellar and with infinite care attached the ends to various valves fixed to the sides of the vats. When satisfied that the connections were secure, pumps from the tanker were switched on, making a subdued humming sound and the transfer of the vat's liquids commenced.

The hours slipped away and it was mid-afternoon before one of the guards tapped on the doors of the bedrooms and when answered asked the various occupants very politely if they would get dressed and come downstairs to a meeting with the Doctor.

Terry with his arm around Lydia's waist was the first down with Jason and Davy following close behind. They entered the kitchen where the doctor was sat, another man sat beside him and they were in deep conversation. They broke off as they came through the doorway. Another armed masked guard stepped to one side as they approached the doorway and then closed the door behind them.

The doctor motioned them to the chairs and when they were all seated, looked at them closely.

"I hope you are all feeling a bit better after your rest." The Doctor looked at Terry.

"I am afraid you may end up with a rather nasty scar on your face, Major. Knowing what I do about you, I doubt if it will bother you too much. It may even make you look more like the pirate, I know you are," he added with a bright smile.

Lydia gave a little giggle at this and squeezed Terry's hand. She had regained much of her composure after her terrible ordeal. The Doctor continued,

"I would like to introduce you to one of my top technicians. For security purposes, I am unable to tell you his real name but you may refer to him as 'Hal'. Suffice to say he is principally engaged in bio medical research at Porton Down but I have temporally withdrawn him from that to concentrate in the situation we have here and report on his finding which at this early stages of the proceedings will only be brief and obviously not a full one, which will take some time to evaluate due to the huge amount of data we now have to process Over to you, Hal."

Hal, a small man of about 40 years old with a slightly receding hair line whose hair was what is commonly known as a 'salt and pepper' colour had grey darting eyes set in a thin, inscrutable looking face. He had the appearance of someone who was not given to humour. He looked around at the group in front of him.

"I have been informed by Dr Faulkner that I am allowed to speak openly to you about what has happened here and also about my preliminary report. We removed what we believed to be the most important items from the cellar first and these were rushed back to Portion Down for analysis. Our immediate findings are most worrying and I fear that further research will only make the matter more so."

He cleared his throat with a slight cough and then continued, "There is no doubt at all that considerable research had been made into the dioxins contained in Agent Orange. Whether or not a complete breakthrough had been made cannot be confirmed at this early stage but in light of what actually transpired here today seems to confirm that for certain they were able to proceed to manufacture some seriously potent and lethal substances."

Hal looked across at Lydia.

"The body of the man who you injected with that serum from the syringe you found was removed with a great deal of care and preliminary investigation has already shown us that his body reacted extremely violently to it. In all of my years of research, I have never seen such a fast reaction with the truly awful consequences to a human body. No doubt the autopsy will reveal more."

Lydia shuddered visibly and smuggled closer to Terry.

Hal continued, "When you bear in mind that as far of we can reasonably know that syringe had been on the floor for possible 20 years, it beggars believe that it would appear that it was originally intended to be injected into someone and if not to kill them, then what or why? This leads onto to another question. It is obvious that someone was kept captive in the second cellar and was apparently kept for experimentation purposes. With a closer look at the shackle which was worn leading on to a break in the chain, I think it is fair to say that someone broke out, resulting in a fight across the main laboratory, possible leading to the death of Harvey Trelease. From what you and the Doctor have already told me, I suspect that the victim is still alive and roaming around this area, above and below ground. Hence your mysterious visitor to your daughter bedroom, Mr Bates being attacked in the tunnels and the Major's experience also in the mines and then hunted across the marsh by this poor creature who views every person in comes across as a threat to its existence. I am sure after its treatment down in the cellars, it would not feel too benevolent to other humans.

"What I do not understand is how it has managed to survive for so long, especially if it had been injected with these dioxins or any derivatives. From what we have so far revealed from some of the hard drives on the computers and what is truly worrying is that we think that Harvey may indeed have had some success in isolating some of these. The problem for us is to what extent he succeeded and if so, where are the results of these tests. I would surmise that the fact that the human victim is at large and that the contents of that syringe would appear to have been about to be used on it. I would suggest that he did actually produce a serum to make a human being biologically and chemically resistant. To what extent is impossible to know at this stage and how this has affected the victim is also unknown.

"For certain the final 'concoction', if you will excuse the word, is not here and that is extremely worrying. This serum, whatever it is, MUST be found and destroyed. If it was to get out to the wider world the repercussions would be terrible. From intelligence information, we have already received, we already know that several foreign countries are experimenting with DNA research and toxins to try to produce a 'super soldier'. If this serum became available to them, it would short cut their research. This could be potentially disastrous to the safety of the western world. I sincerely hope you all realise just how lucky you have been. I repeat. We must find it! To coin a phrase once the genie has escaped from the bottle it will be impossible to put it back."

"Thank you, Hal", said the Doctor looking around at all of them in turn.

"Now! On to your daughter, Major. We have found no sign of her at all and can only guess that either she had left the house prior to your visitors, which seems unlikely or which is more likely she saw or heard what was going down with you and decided to hide in the only place she knew they would not find her and that is in the hidden tunnel behind the fireplace. My team have done a preliminary search but you are correct, Major. It's like a rabbit warren down there and I just do not have the manpower to conduct a complete search, especially now that we know this being that is down there is potentially very violent and extremely strong." The Doctor paused. "I really am so sorry. Just as soon as we can – we will!"

Tears welled up in Lydia's eyes while Terry, Jason and Davy looked grim.

"Anyway, we will be pulling out shortly and will return to Portion Down with the remainder of the recovered equipment to further investigate. Everything that has been left in the cellars has been certified safe, not that there is much remaining. The bulk of it has been removed.

"I have asked for a police patrol to be left at the top of your driveway and I will leave two of my men to guard the house.

"You and Davy may be surprised how much you have in common with them!"

The Doctor's eyes twinkled somewhat mischievously as though he had knowledge of a hidden joke.

He rose to go and shook the hands of all present.

"I hope you all realise that officially, none of this actually happened. Obviously no action will be taken against you, Mrs Knight or you, Mr Bates, regarding the demise of or two unwelcome visitors." They both looked relieved at this.

"We will find your daughter, Mrs Knight, of that I am sure. I will have a team on it first thing but for now, goodbye. Stay safe."

Hal follow him out to the waiting Range Rover and climbed into the rear seat with the Doctor. An armed guard slid into the front passenger seat. The engine purred and gravel spurted from the tyres as it accelerated away up the driveway. The only vehicles that remained were another black range rover belonging to the two guards left behind and Terry's Volvo. The car belonging to the two deceased thugs had been removed for forensic examination. Apparently, the police had already confirmed that it had been stolen a few weeks previously from a neighbouring town, this information in itself was a little worrying at it meant that plans appeared to have been made at that time to enter the house and possibly blow up the cellars. The two men's identify was still a mystery as no record could so far be found of them entering the country. Further investigation was to continue according to Dr Faulkner but at this stage it was thought they had been illegal immigrants who had come in through the country's currently very porous border.

Lydia busied herself in the kitchen and in short order came up with several plates of food for they were all hungry, not having eaten for the day.

Davy looked around at them and then fixed his eyes on Terry.

"When do you want to start, Boss?" he said quietly.

Terry returned his look with hooded eyes and took another bite out of his ham and cheese sandwich.

"Just as soon as I have eaten this, we can go. Jason, you are to stay and look after your mother. No arguments, there's a good lad," as Jason opened his mouth to protest.

"Davy, you still got your little bag of tricks, haven't you? If so, go and get it."

Davy nodded silently and left the room. As he did so, the armed guard who had been patrolling outside in the corridor entered the kitchen. He saluted Terry. "I'm sorry, Major, but I could not help but overhear what you just said. I have strict orders to stay alongside you, sir, so if it is OK with you, I wish to come with you!"

Terry stared hard at the man but something suddenly twitched in his mind.

“I know you, don’t I? You may have a mask on but I know your voice. I never forget a voice!”

The guard responded by slowly rolling up the balaclava covering his face. As it cleared his head, a wide smile appeared which played around his lips. He straightened his shoulders and snapped to attention and saluted Terry again.

“You sure do, Major, sir. You sure do!”

At that moment, Davy returned and his eyes widened in surprise as he took in the scene.

“Bloody hell! As I live and die. Kyle! You old mucker! I thought there was something familiar about you but couldn’t put a handle on it!”

Kyle grinned.

“Good to see you too, Davy. It has been a while.”

Terry looked across at Lydia and Jason and explained,

“Kyle is the guy who led our section out of harm’s way while I went back for Davy!”

Kyle smile vanished.

“I lost two of your best men that night, Major and I will always remember them and wish things could have been different but at least we brought them home with us.”

“If you hadn’t of contacted our base and organised our LZ, they would not have even known where to start looking for us. Especially with our comms gone to hell and back.”

Terry stared grimly.

“It was an amazing bit of work what with that blood thirsty mob tracking your every move and bearing in mind, you were outnumbered by at least 10–1.”

“My sorts of odds, Major,” Kyle said with a slight grin.

Terry’s eyes flickered.

“So this is a Group operation and this is what Dr Faulkner meant with his little joke about how much we may have in common!”

Kyle nodded.

“When the Doctor told us it was you, I couldn’t wait to see you again, sir. He also said I was to stay with you when you go to search for your daughter. He knew you would go before a suitable team could be put together sir!” Kyle stood to attention again.

“So Dr Faulkner is a member of Group?”

“Not just a member, sir. He is on the committee. One of the top honchos, who decides on life or death for our enemies.”

“My God! I never would have thought it. He is so unassuming but then, I suppose it is part of his cover.”

Terry stood up and grimaced with pain. This quickly washed away as his thoughts turned to Natasha.

“It is decided then. So, let’s go!”

* * * * *

Chapter Sixteen
Instructions

The phone rang only twice before it was snatched up.

"Yes?" The man listened intently.

"Nothing? That should have been impossible. Something is seriously wrong. The whole place should have been destroyed by now and you now tell me the police have now put a road block on the entrance drive? And what of Faulkner? He was there?"

"That interfering bastard Knight and his miserable family should have gone up with it."

"Can't your men get anything right?" he screamed down the phone.

"Yes, of course, we go tonight. Nothing had better go wrong with that! I do not accept failure. You know that. I will meet you there myself. Make sure you bring enough men. If you want to live, make it happen."

The phone was slammed down.

The man wiped the perspiration away from his forehead and standing up, walked over to a large filling cabinet which stood against the wall.

Taking a small bunch of keys from his pocket, he selected one and entered it into the lock. It gave a slight click and he slid the top drawer open. He removed the files which it contained and placed them on a desk beside the cabinet. Placing his hand down firmly on the base of the drawer, he pushed ever so slightly down. The base moved revealing a space beneath from which he removed a semi-automatic pistol together with several spare clips of ammunition which was hidden in the recess.

His eyes turned to slits behind his glasses.

"Now you just get in my way again, Mr bloody Major Knight and it will be the last thing you ever do!"

He tucked the gun into his waist band and picked up the thick waterproof anorak which hung from a hook on the door. Putting it on, he then took the bunch of keys and slid them into his pocket. He collected a brief case as he left the building by a side door which led into a garage containing a very smart BMW sports car. Starting the engine he pressed the key fob and the garage door retracted into the ceiling. He would be early. It wasn't too far. He would not be returning!

* * * * *

Chapter Seventeen
The Cave

Natasha inched her way through the pitch-black tunnel. She had fallen over several times due to the uneven floor and the darkness. She knew her knees were bleeding slightly as she could feel her hot blood dripping down the front of her knees.

So much for her false nails, she thought to herself as her hands scrabbled against the rough rock walls. She lost track of time but a few hours must have elapsed since she trapped herself.

Suddenly, she felt herself falling. Too late to prevent it, she landed with a thud and continued to roll down a steep slope. She crashed to a stop but her head flicked over to thump against a protruding rock. Unconsciousness came quickly.

The first thing she was aware of was a stinging pain to her head. She went to raise it and let out a groan. Raising her hand, she touched her forehead and to her surprise felt a bandage around it. Very slowly, she felt around and realised she was lying on what appeared to be a flat slab of rock covered with fluffy animal skins. She strained her eyes into the darkness which surrounded her and then went to sit up, swinging her legs over the side of the rocky ledge.

Something moved close to her, a slight scuffing sound. She recoiled in terror.

"Who is there? What do you want?"

"Drink!"

A single word spoken in a crackling muffled voice and a cup was pushed into her hands, liquid splashed over her fingers. She raised the cup and sipped the contents. Ice cold water. She drank greedily until it was finished. It wasn't as dark as before and she made out a large figure standing in front of her silhouetted against a backdrop of grey light which filtered in from beyond. With it came the sound of the sea, the thundering of surf crashing and cascading on the rocks. Natasha could smell the salt of the air and with it a slight animal type of smell like the sort of smell you would get from a dog that had got wet and you were drying it off with a towel. Slightly musty but not overly unpleasant.

"You are safe."

The voice crackled again.

"No harm will come to you while I am here."

"Who are you?" Natasha whispered. There was a slight pause and then a rasping snort.

"You could say I am, to certain men, their worst nightmare come to life. But to you, I will be YOUR life and nobody will hurt you. I have watched you sleep and listened to you laugh. You make me feel alive. Something I have not felt before during my poor miserable existence. You will be mine." The voice rasped on.

Natasha felt a shiver run down her back.

"You were in my bedroom? You touched me?" Her voice rising. She knew the answer before she asked the question. There was no doubt.

The cave was lightening rapidly now and she could now make out more clearly the figure which had crouched down in front of her. Natasha put her hand to her head which throbbed unmercifully and closed her eyes hoping that her vision might clear as the face of the figure seemed to blur and the features of the face turned liquid and contorted. She slowly opened her eyes again and realised with a growing horror that she was not dreaming. The huge man in front of her had the most distorted and twisted face she had ever seen in her life. It was barely human, so deformed was it. Hair sprouted in tuffs from the skin and head, long and dank. It was dressed in skins which barely covered a monstrous body. Muscles bulged across the shoulders and its thick misshapen neck. Sharp, uneven teeth sprouted from a gash in its mouth which was twisted to one side and the nose above it was flattened with broad nostrils, one of which was higher than the other. The ears were harder to see, covered as they were in the thick coarse hair but appeared to be much larger than normal with the tips of them splayed out almost at right angles to the head. It slowly extended a huge hand out towards Natasha, who recoiled in total terror. It was more similar to a claw than a human hand, callused, rough and misshapen. At the end of its fingers, long sharp black nails were extended with a thick growth of dark hair all over the skin.

The light was rapidly strengthening and Natasha was aware of its eyes which were bright, clear blue, staring intently at her from beneath bushy eyebrows.

The voice crackled again but very softly. "The last thing I want to do is to frighten you. I know I look hideous and this is a terrible shock to you but I really do not mean you any harm. I have never been able to talk to anyone of my feelings of being so ugly since my mother died when I was young. I am so…" He paused and then in a voice to low that Natasha had to strain her ears to hear it. "Lonely."

An eye glistened and a tear ran slowly down the terrible face.

Natasha suddenly had a feeling of great sympathy and sorrow for this beast of a man before her like she had never felt before. She looked around the large cave and realised it was completely dry. Numerous skins lay around on the floor and some attempt had been made to fashion some rough chairs made from what appeared to be driftwood alongside some planks of the same which had been made into a table. Some kitchen utensils were laid out on top of it. A hearth had been constructed with a pile of large stones, blackened with soot and with some large logs smouldering away in the centre, the tendrils of smoke rising up and then disappearing in the high roof vault of the cave. A number of pots surrounded the fire with one hanging from a hook suspended with a metal rod in the middle of the fire. Some slabs of meat also hung from hooks fixed to the wall of the rock.

Natasha stood up and slowly walked towards the light now streaming in from the end of the cave. She came out onto a ledge a hundred feet up on the side of the cliff. The edge dropped sheer to the sea which pulsed with a life of its own as it foamed and cascaded over the glistening rocks at the bottom over a hundred feet below. She looked up and the cliffs rose completely sheer above her. With a slight shock, she suddenly realised where she was. She could see the old mine stack standing stark and tall in the morning light on the top of the cliffs opposite to her. She remembered Jason's description of the ledge below him on the opposite point where he had thought he had seen a figure during the storm and his story of hearing a long moaning cry which he could not identify. His eyes had not deceived him. He obviously had seen something.

"There is no way up or down from here," the voice said and she was aware that he had followed her out onto the ledge and was standing directly behind her. "And the caves leading off from the cavern are numerous, complex and many quite dangerous and very easy to get lost or die in."

The shape beside gazed into the distance.

"Reckon, there is another storm coming in again. A bad one by the look of the swell."

Natasha shivered as this had been said in such matter of fact way, she could not doubt the truth of what he had said.

"How did you come to be imprisoned down here?" she asked.

"Imprisoned? No, not imprisoned. Kept safe and away from prying and nasty humans." The man gave a sort of muffled snort. "I was born down here nearly 20 years ago. My mother was a beautiful woman who looked after me as well as anyone could under the circumstances. She was kind and thoughtful and took a lot of care to try to teach me things. But when I was about 12 years old, some very bad men came into the caves. They sprayed a gas into the tunnels. My father appeared to be immune to it but I was very ill for a while and eventually recovered. My mother was not strong enough to withstand it and died soon afterwards. I still miss her!" The voice trembled slightly and something similar to a sob escaped from deep inside his chest.

"What happened to the men?"

Natasha turned around to face him. He stood there, head bowed, shoulders shaking slightly with emotion, tears dripping of the ragged hairs on his face. For all the horror of her situation, she could not but help to feel sorrow for this creature which towered over her. She suddenly realised that he was about her age.

"My father's rage was a terrible thing to see. They never saw him coming. Never realised anyone could have survived the gas. He killed both of them. What he did to them before they died was not good to see but they deserved it. He threw what was left of their bodies into the sea from here. When I recovered, we revered her in our cavern of caverns. She is still there. I go to talk to her from time to time. It helps me."

"Where is your father now?"

"Oh! He is near but do not fear him. He will respect my wishes. You may find him…difficult to look at. He has his demons inside his head."

Natasha shivered again, involuntary.

He coughed and straightened up. "Come, you must rest. I have been preparing a place for you. Sleep while I cook some food." He pressed a hand against her back and guided her back into the cave and along a side passage, where a blanket hung across the entrance. Pulling it to one side, he allowed her to enter, more furs were piled onto another flat rock slab and then to Natasha's amazement, she recognised a pile of her own clothes. "So this is where they went! You stole them from my room. And I blamed Jason for moving them."

"Shh, now! Lie down and sleep." He pushed her over to the furs and made her lie down before covering her with the skins. They actually felt good and a great feeling of weariness overcame her. Her head throbbed. She closed her eyes and within minutes was fast asleep.

He drew the blanket back across the opening and went back to the fire where he filled the cooking pot with some slabs of meat, added some green leaves and poured some water over the top. Engrossed in his task, he failed to notice someone else until his shoulder was grasped in a vice like grip.

"Where is she?" the voice low and mumbled.

"Sleeping!"

"They will come to take her back," the voice rumbled again.

"You know that, don't you?"

"The others will come again too! They will not let us rest until they have the flasks. Just let them have them, Father."

"Never. They will all die." He let out a deep breath and a low resonant moan echoed around the cavern.

Hands clenched and unclenched nails if you could call them that, scrapped against each other.

"They will die."

* * * * *

Chapter Eighteen
Collison Course

The wind was raging and the rain came down in sheets, obscuring the valley as the full might of another low depression from the Atlantic raced in. Night had come early, caused in part by the black, scudding clouds. Inside the house, Terry, Davy and Kyle were checking over their equipment. This time, however, they were all dressed in waterproofs. Jason and Lydia looked on with worried expressions on their faces.

Terry slid an arm around Lydia and kissed her. "Don't worry. We will find her and bring her back safely. Just you see!"

Lydia squeezed his arm and her eyes moistened with tears.

They all trooped up to Natasha's bedroom and Terry went to the fireplace and opened up the hidden doorway. Silently, the three men filed into the passageway behind, flicking on their torches as they did so. As the last one passed through, the door gave a faint rumble and closed behind them.

They followed the passage for a while and then it divided and after a short distance, divided again. Not wanting to take any chances of getting lost this time, Terry kept marking the rock walls to indicate which way they proceeded.

The tunnels sometimes split into numerous entrances, some even going up into what appeared to be higher levels and then again, into lower ones. Some, so narrow, that they had difficulty in squeezing through. In others, they had to crawl through as the roof was so low and then again, sometimes it heightened into huge caverns. The tunnels seemed endless. Water dripped down incessantly making the floor slippery. Progress was slow. Entering yet another cavern, Davy suddenly pointed to a pile of rotting, wooden stakes with some very old mining tools stacked against the cave wall.

"I've been in this cave before," he stated. "I recognise those. I passed through here before I found the way to the cellar. We must be heading away from the house and going towards the sea and cliffs."

"Yes, and still no sign of Natasha," said Terry grimly.

Davy slapped Terry's arm. "We'll find her, Boss, don't you worry now."

Terry just grunted. He was obviously in considerable pain. The fractured ribs and the injuries to his ankle were taking their toll on him, plus the stress of trying to find Natasha. He turned and limped after Kyle down yet another tunnel, Davy behind him. A short while later, the tunnel suddenly steepened and they slipped and slithered down the gradient.

Reaching the bottom, Kyle stopped and held up his hand to indicate everyone to stop. He bent down and picked up something from the ground. He held out his clenched hand to Terry and slowly opened his fingers. Something glistened in the palm of his hand. "Recognise this, Boss," he asked.

Terry stared at it and gave a grin. "It's one of Natasha's earrings. We gave them to her on her birthday. That great! Now we know she came this way."

Kyle did not share in Terry's enthusiasm and was staring intently at the floor.

"Someone else was here. Look, in the mud."

They peered at the ground. There, outlined in a small slick of mud, was a large footprint. Terry had a troubled look on his face but said nothing. They pressed on along the narrow tunnel. After several more turnings they heard the rush of water and come out onto a large ledge overhanging the raging torrent.

"It was near here where that thing knocked me into the water!" Davy exclaimed. *Except that, well, it is not quite the same somehow. I've got it! We are on the other side of it and I think a bit further down the ravine. How in hell did we manage to do that?* He thought for a minute. "The river must come out of the rocks somewhere up river and we must have crossed over the top of it without realising it." He had to raise his voice to make himself heard over the roaring water.

"We have to keep going," Terry shouted. "Follow the path."

They proceed to the far end of the ledge and the labyrinth of tunnels continued. The sound of the river had dulled to a low murmur in the distance. Kyle was still leading with Terry following painfully behind him and again Davy bringing up the rear. Kyle stopped, raising his arm with a clenched fist, so abruptly that Terry almost collided with him.

They all stood there motionless, listening and straining their eyes into the darkness.

"What is it?" Terry whispered to Kyle.

"I thought I heard voices," he whispered back. "There! I was right."

Terry tried to push past him. "Natasha."

"Wait, Boss! More than one! Several!"

They crept forward and shortly turned a sharp bend in the tunnel. More voices could be heard up ahead and a slight glow emanated from the tunnel ahead. Kyle motioned to them to turn off their head torches. They slowly and carefully slid forward as the light became brighter. The tunnel terminated above a large cavern which was brightly lit with floodlights casting deep shadows along its sides. They crawled to the edge of rocks at the leading exit of the tunnel and looked down in amazement at the scene below them. The scene was illuminated by two large flood lights and evidently powered by a small generator, which purred away gently in the corner. A set of narrow gauge railway lines crossed the floor of the cavern and disappeared into one of the tunnels. The cavern was lined with steel racks, some empty but others containing row upon row of small flasks which were being withdrawn very carefully from the shelves by a group of men, who were loading them into small wheeled cages. As they watched, two men pushed one of the full cages along the rails across the cavern floor and disappeared into another tunnel on the far side.

Several men stood around the periphery holding guns at the ready. They looked nervous as if they were expecting trouble.

"What do we do now, Boss?" Davy whispered.

"How many men can you count?" Terry whispered back.

Kyle hesitated for a few seconds before answering. "I make it eight plus the two who have just left. It looks like only four of them are armed. But what on earth is going on here?"

"I think we have just found the reason for all of the grief we have experienced. Somehow, this looks like the end product of all the experimentation. There must be another exit close by and they are moving the gear. We must stop them. We will have to take them out. Check your weapons."

They moved quietly, checking the magazines and slipping the safety catches off.

"If we slowly creep down and around the edge, keeping as much as possible to the shadows, we may be able to surprise them. Only move when they make some noise. In that bright light, they will probably have dark blindness and not be able to see beyond the lights to much extent. I will give them just one warning to surrender and if they don't comply immediately, then take out the armed men first and shoot to kill. I do not intend to mess around with these guys." Terry instructed.

Kyle crawled off the left, Davy to the right. Terry intended to slip over the lip of the rocks once his men were in position and go straight down.

Kyle and Davy signalled that they were ready. Terry readied himself. He raised his automatic and fired into the roof. The bullet whined off into the distance and at the same time he shouted down at the men below. "Put your guns down. You are surrounded. NOW!"

The reaction was instant. All four of the armed men wheeled around and commenced firing in Terry's direction, who had now ducked out of sight behind a huge boulder. Chips of stone showered down on him. Gunfire erupted in all directions. Kyle and Davy fired back and instantly two of the guards went down and didn't move. Confusion reigned in the cavern. The other two armed men dived for cover, one tripping over the cable attached to one of the floodlights bringing it crashing down. There was a flash and the light went out. He tried to scramble up but his foot was caught in a loop of the cable. Terry sliding down the slope towards him, took aim, fired but his aim was slightly off because of the uneven rocks which jolted his arm. The bullet caught the guard high in the chest and he toppled over backwards. He struggled to his knees and desperately tried to swing his gun around to bear as Terry shot him again, this time catching him right in the centre of his forehead. He slumped over and didn't move. Eyes wide open. The remaining guard threw his weapon down and the other four men stood up with their hands in the air.

Terry covered them with his gun as Kyle and Davy joined him on the floor of the cavern with big grins on their faces.

Kyle beamed at Terry. "That went well."

Terry just grunted. Sweat dripped of his face. He clutched his side in pain. Davy looked at him with concern.

"You hit, Boss?"

"No! Just my ribs. I twisted myself as I slid down the slope."

Terry turned to look at their captives. "Davy, pat them down, will you? I don't want any nasty surprises."

Davy hurried to comply but as he approached the remaining guard, from behind them, two shots boomed out, echoing around the cave. Terry and Davy swung around. Three more guards fanned out of the tunnel which the cage had disappeared into, waving their automatic weapons at them.

Terry turned to find Kyle. He was standing a short distance away in a crouched position. Terry looked in horror as he very slowly crumbled to the ground, one his hands clutching the side of his neck. Blood bubbled out between his fingers.

He gagged and more blood dribbled out of his mouth. He slid to his knees. His chin dropped to rest on his chest. "Booooss." The words were barely audible. A burst of blood splattered onto the rocks from his open mouth. Then, he didn't move again.

"Put your gun down, Davy. We are heavily outnumbered."

For a moment, Terry thought Davy was not going to follow his order. Davy stood there, his face working with emotion.

"Davy! Just do it!"

Davy, very slowly, let his gun slip from his grasp and it clattered to the ground.

The original remaining guard bent down and retrieved his weapon and then took up a position with the three other men to surround Terry and Davy. The others, with only a passing glance at them, went back to work on moving the flasks.

A sound of clapping hands broke the silence. A man stood at the entrance to the tunnel.

"Well done, Major Terry! Well done! So good to see you again and the nice Captain Bates as well. Well, this is a surprise. We all had expected never to see you again. But, then, life is always full of surprises, isn't it?"

Terry slowly turned towards him. “I was waiting to see when you were going to crawl out of the woodwork. I just knew you would turn up sooner or later, Dr Jackson or should I call you by your real name – Dr Kevin Brent?”

“Ah! So you worked it out then?”

“It wasn’t too difficult. You kept on turning up just a little too often where you shouldn’t. No doubt you will dispose of us where nobody will ever find our bodies.”

“Hmmm! Not sure about that. I might just leave you to our absent friend to deal with you. It might just be easier, more tidy if you get my drift.” He laughed unpleasantly.

“In that case you may as well fill me in the details of how you managed to get to this point, seeing as we are never going to be able to tell anyone,” said Terry.

Dr Jackson stroked his chin. “May as well, I suppose. I am really proud of what we have achieved even though it took a lot longer than we ever expected. I think it started when the delightful Dr Faulkner found out what Trelease and I were really doing in the labs. We were on the brink of a major breakthrough to produce a serum which could be administered to a range of men to make them immune to any sort of biological or germ warfare products known to mankind. Then he sacked us. He threw us out on the rubbish pile as though we were not worth anything.” He practically spat out the last sentence, his voice rising until he was screaming, drops of spittle forming around his mouth.

Terry realised that he was on the edge of mania and was all the more dangerous because of it and decided to play up to his ego.

“You must have been a brilliant pair of scientists to do this.”

"We were, we were! And we had the ambition to do what others were not prepared to do. We had to start all over again but luckily I found a sponsor who was prepared to finance our research."

"When you were in Korea?"

"Oh! You know about that, then?"

"Faulkner told me they had tracked you there and then disappeared."

"Ha! The fool! I came back with a new identity, unlimited funding to assist Trelease. He inherited this place which with money, we converted it to our rather special needs. By the time I returned, he had organised things very well indeed. He had prepared a subject and had already commenced testing."

"Where did he get his subject from without arousing suspicion," interjected Terry.

"He found a young gipsy girl and a lad who he forced to make her pregnant. In the initial experiments and injections, the girl died before the baby was born but he didn't give up."

"Oh, no! He found another girl and with the improvements in the various injections given to both parents, the baby was born which we then raised in the cellar."

"What did you do with parents?"

"They were disposed of. We had no further use for them. It was all about the baby. This is where we had gone wrong the first time."

"So you kidnapped three innocent people, incarcerated them in this hell hole, probably tortured them with all sorts of injection until you had finished with them, then you murdered them in cold blood? You blood thirsty swine!" Terry could no longer conceal his fury, clenching and unclenching his fists at the thought of the lack of compassion.

Jackson or Brent as was his real name, looked at Terry in surprise.

"I would have thought you, of all people, would have appreciated the effort we put in to achieve our aim. To make a country's army invincible! It was for scientific research. They died to help mankind. They were martyred, to be remembered forever. Their sacrifice will not be in vain. They were heroes even if they didn't know it," Brent ranted on.

We reared the baby and it grew into everything we had hoped for and more. It was amazing! Its hearing, its sensory ability, the sheer size of the brute, its muscular strength, its ability to see in almost total darkness. Everything about it exceeded our wildest expectations.

We continued with the injections and then extracted its blood to develop a serum. Then we experienced problems because the serum needed time to multiply and grow and could only do this in a very stable temperature. Also, we needed a lot of it as we had to create enough to inject an army. We found that the cavern down here was big enough to store everything. It was perfect! The temperature of this cavern does not vary more than a degree or two all the year around and was reasonably dry. Also, we had the track which runs right from underneath the laboratory, right up to the other shaft exit underneath the old mine pump house. We could store the flasks in perfect safety down here until it had 'matured'.

"Oh! And then disaster! It escaped, didn't it? You didn't expect that, did you?" Terry sneered.

"That was very, eh, unfortunate. Trelease got attacked and his injuries were so severe, he died virtually immediately. I managed to get him out and lock this creature in the lab. I thought it would die down there, especially as it would not get its injections and then we could finish everything up and clear out. But this was not to be. Somehow, it found a way out and into the mines. They stretch for miles and there are several levels of them, some connected and some not.

“Eventually, my friends and I organised things to try and remove the flasks when we thought they would have reached maturity. They entered through the mine shaft pump house, the same as we have done, just to check, you understand. It wasn’t until they were found on the beach along here, dead and badly mutilated that we realised this thing was still very much alive.

“I had realised it had got outside because of when old man Harry rushed up to Trelease House to get me to attend to Mr Winston on the cliff path on that same fateful day that it killed Trelease. However, I never thought it could survive for long.

“Later, we sent another team in to make sure it was dead and if not, kill it with poison gas. That didn’t work either. We had done our job too well. They ended up on the beach dead as well.” Brent shuddered. “I had to do an autopsy on them. It was horrific! They had been mutilated way beyond recognition. Then we kept getting reports, only vague ones, of sightings and unusual noises especially at night. The local people avoided this area like the plague, which suited us really well.

“I needed to keep an eye on things here so I moved into the house intending to live here until we could recover the flasks.”

“Oh! My God! So I actually bought the house from you!” exclaimed Terry.

Brent laughed. "You have no idea how funny we thought this was to start with but then we did not know who you were then, did we, Major? Or of your connections shall we say?"

"Why did you leave? Why sell it?" asked Davy.

Brent spat onto the ground. "The bloody thing must have realised I was living there. It kept on trying to break in at night. That is why I installed all those heavy grills across the windows. It kept it out but I knew that eventually it would one day catch me off guard and try to kill me, so I moved out to the town and abandoned the place until we were ready in sufficient numbers to remove the flasks. Our work was done. We just needed to wait for the serum to multiply naturally."

"So this poor creature, which knows no better, is after your blood and in the process kills or is responsible for numerous fatalities and presumably was responsible for killing old man Harry. This all lies at your door Brent, you bloody butcher, all in the name of science. Not for the money, oh, no! You wouldn't have thought of that, would you?" Terry proclaimed.

"Yes, it was a shame about Harry. I actually liked him. He was in the wrong place and at the wrong time. It may have mistaken him for me. I had given him an old coat of mine some days before when he had turned up at the surgery soaking wet because the coat he was wearing leaked."

"So, because he smelt like you, it killed him?" Terry snorted.

"Hmm! Yes, something like that, I think. It was obviously feeding itself on his sheep. He was always moaning about how he had lost some." Brent laughed again.

"Anyway, it is now all done except how we deal with you. The flasks will be out of the country by tomorrow and in a few days, I will be taking a well-earned rest and will be able to live the rest of my life in extreme luxury.

"I think we may just tie you up to await our rather large furry friend. It seems a shame not to let it have some fun in its life.

"To make sure of it, I will even give you my new coat to wear. Ha! Ha!"

With that, Brent started to undo the zip to his anorak. Just as he was doing this, there was an almighty crash and the remaining flood light tipped over and smashed, instantly plunging the cavern into total darkness but not before Terry and Davy had a fleeting glimpse of a huge terrifying figure leaping off the rocky shelf directly behind Brent and landing on his shoulders. Brent screamed in agony as he collapsed onto the floor. His gun went off randomly, briefly illuminating the scene with the flash.

Terry and Davy dropped to the ground and scrabbled through the rocks, desperately trying to find their guns. Brent screamed again and they heard the sound of bones breaking and of something tearing and ripping at his flesh. All the time, there was this low resonant sound of moaning, which chilled the blood. Random gunfire ripped across the cavern. The guards were firing in all direction, totally indiscriminately, unable to see what was happening. More screams rang out, a brief pause and then a hoarse shout. Then again more sounds of crunching and moaning.

"Keep down," Terry whispered to Davy. "I will see if I can find our lights."

"I've found the guns," Davy whispered back. Terry continued to search the area and suddenly his fingers touched something which he didn't immediately recognise.

"I've found your bag," Terry said with relief.

"I think there may be some flares left."

Terry groped around and his hand closed around a stick like object. He pulled it out and gripped the top and wrenched it off. A second delay and then it fizzed into life, illuminating the cavern in ghostly white light. A picture of total carnage was revealed. Only one of the guards was still standing and he was retreating back into one the tunnels waving his gun and firing it at anything that moved. Briefly, they glimpsed the figures of two of the workers behind him staggering back through the tunnel, disappearing into the blackness. One of the fallen guards cried out and tried to stand up. He caught a bullet in the middle of his chest and collapsed over backwards. The remaining armed guard retreated back into the tunnel and disappeared from view.

Something else moved. It looked at first as if it was just a pile of furs. Then it slowly stood up. Terry looked at it in horror.

It stood a full 7' tall, tangled and matted hair hung down from its head like a lion's mane. Blood and gore was splattered all down its front with some pieces of flesh stuck in it its uneven jaws. More tatters of flesh hung from the huge malformed claws at the end of what appeared to be its hands. A massive heavily muscled chest, covered in coarse hair protruded from a shoulder covered in fur. It raised a limb and covered its eyes. Terry realised instantly that the bright light was hurting it and it was struggling to focus.

A really loud moaning sound issued from its throat and it turned its head towards Terry and Davy. The face was hideously deformed from what could be seen of it through the hair. The head was slowly raised and it snuffled at the air. Its face wrinkled up, bared its teeth and gave forth a terrifying snarl. Mucus dripped from its uneven nostrils. Now shuffling slowly towards them on its monstrous misshapen legs, squinting against the light, it had a murderous intent in the way it moved. Kevin Brent lay on the rocky floor in a pool of blood, his head had been nearly severed from his shoulders. His chest and stomach blooded and ripped. Some his entrails had spilled out of his lower abdomen in a cascade of grey coils.

Another even louder moan echoed around the cavern.

Terry raised his automatic and levelled it at this ghastly vision.

"Stop! Or I will shoot you," he shouted. "Stop, I say!"

20 feet away now and still coming. 15 feet.

"Boss! Shoot the fucking thing. It's going to kill us. You can see it in its eyes," Davy screamed.

10 feet and not stopping. Terry fired. Saw the bullet hit. The creature staggered slightly but kept coming. He fired again without any appreciative effect. Davy opened up with his automatic as well. Bullets splattered into its chest. Terry could feel the hot breath from its nostrils and a claw extended towards him when he raised his gun again and fired straight into the misshapen forehead.

A gurgled cry rang out. It staggered back and collapsed at Terry's feet.

"Bloody hell! What the fuck is that?" Davy exclaimed.

Terry was breathing very heavily, stepped back a pace and looked down at this almost alien creature lying at his feet.

He ran a hand across his face somewhat wearily.

"I think it just wanted revenge on Brent for the pain he and Trelease inflicted on its' poor miserable existence and the suffering it had at their hands in the laboratory. Once it tasted blood, it would go on and kill anything that got in its way.

"What a creature! I almost feel sorry for it. I just wish we had not had to kill it. Look at the size of it. Just imagine if we had to fight a war in Bio suits against an army of these creatures who would be impervious to biological and chemical weapons. It doesn't bear thinking about."

"Well, it made short work of Brent. Jesus Christ! Look at the state of him all in less time than it took to blink. The poor bugger has been nearly torn in two. Ugh," said Davy.

"Anyway, what now, Boss?"

They stared in silence for a moment or two. Davy shook his head as if to rid his eyes of the gruesome sight.

The flare was now nearly out but it still had enough light for them to see the chaotic scene surrounding them across the cavern. They both flicked on their headlights.

"We must follow the rails and try to stop this stuff leaving the country. Finding Natasha will have to wait," said Terry grimly.

Davy looked at Terry and realised the mental turmoil he was experiencing. Apart from the pain Davy knew he must be in from his various injuries over the past few days and the stress of trying to protect his family. To look for your daughter or save your country from the possibility of the terrible repercussions that could happen if this serum became available to a hostile country? In this uncertain world, there were plenty enough of them to worry about. This was not even thinking about what could happen if it fell into the hands of terrorists. THAT was possibly even a worse scenario. Not a decision to be taken lightly and he was glad he did not have to make that sort of choice.

"We follow the rails and stop them," Terry said with a determined face. "Let's go."

There was nothing they could do for the people lying dead around the cavern. They carefully made their way across the rocky floor and with their weapons at the ready, slowly entering the tunnel, following the rails set in the floor. The tunnel ran fairly straight for a short distance and then curved around to the left. Various other tunnels joined the one they were following. As they rounded, the bend a burst of automatic fire had them diving for cover. Sharp chips of rock peppered their bodies and bullets whined away into the distance. They caught the glimpse of flashes of light from the guns coming from the next bend.

"Put your headlight out, Davy. We are too obvious a target," Terry muttered as he turned his own off.

"Leave it to me, Boss," Davy turned as he groped in his bag. He gave a grunt of satisfaction as he found what he was looking for. He held a cylindrical object in his hand.

"Leave this to me!"

"Watch out for your ears and eyes, Boss. This is a Bomber Bates special." And gave a short laugh. He fumbled around in his bag again and came out with a type of wide barrelled but stubby pistol. He pushed the end of the cylinder into the barrel with a faint click and pointed it up the tunnel. There was a sudden whoosh as he squeezed the trigger and it sailed off into the distance.

As soon as he had fired, he drop flat onto the ground and covered his head with his arms with his hands jammed into his ears.

The tunnel up ahead exploded into a kaleidoscope of brilliant colours, turning into an inferno of white light from the residual magnesium burning. The blast from the explosion washed over them, hurling dust and debris over them.

"Good God, Davy! What the hell did you put in that?" Terry gasped as he slowly stood up and brushed himself down.

Davy gave bit of a giggle. "Oh, just a bit of this and a bit of that! Something I have been working on for quite a while. Sort of a cross between a flash bang and a mini rocket propelled grenade, guaranteed to upset the ungodly. First time I have actually used it for real. It seems to have worked OK!"

Terry was sure that he was smirking in the darkness which had returned and appeared to be even denser than before.

The shooting had stopped abruptly after the light show and explosion. There was a sound of shouting in the distance and then some screaming. Suddenly, there were several long bursts of firing, another scream and more shouting, which slowly faded away. Silence ensued.

Terry and Davy peered around the corner.

"What the hell were they shooting at?" Terry said frowning.

"It certainly wasn't at us."

They carefully continued further up the tunnel and arrived at the spot where the firing had come from. Some items of singed clothing lay scattered around and there was some evidence that at least one person had been injured, judging from some splashes of blood on the floor.

"Well, Davy, your homemade anti-personal weapon seems to have worked a treat," Terry muttered as he gazed around.

"We can't be!" Terry stopped mid-sentence. Hairs at the back of his neck hardened. From some distance away, a low resonant sound echoed through the tunnel ending with a muted howl.

"What the hell! It can't be! That fucking thing is dead. We shot it, didn't we? It couldn't have possibly survived, could it?" Terry asked Davy.

"No way, Boss. Just some of our friends up ahead playing silly buggers with us, I think."

The sound was not repeated but it was enough to send a prickle of alarm up through both of their spines. It had a horrible, malicious tone to it.

"Let's crack on."

They crept along the passageway, following the rails set in the floor. A short distance along the tunnel, it was joined by another. They peered into the stygian darkness. As there did not appear to be any more resistance, they were able to switch their headlights on again. Something was on the ground just inside the side tunnel. Terry went to see what is was. A body! He gave it a push with his foot and it partially rolled over. Terry jumped back in horror. One arm had been almost entirely ripped off and the face was smashed to a bloody pulp making it completely unrecognisable. Blood had sprayed all over the nearby rocks.

"Jesus Christ!" he exclaimed.

"What the hell did that?"

Davy peered at the corpse.

"Well, whatever it was, it definitely was not my rocket. Look, no powder burns and no bullet wounds. Maybe this was what all the uproar was about. Someone really did not like him, that's for sure. When crooks fall out, etcetera, etcetera."

"Someone sure fired a lot of ammo in this area. Look at all the cartridge cases," Terry said, examining the ground. He rubbed his chin and leant wearily against the rock wall.

"I don't understand it! Still, we better press on."

They moved on down the tunnel, much faster now that they could see the ground ahead with the aid of their headlights which help to speed up their progress. After a few hundred yards or so, the tunnel and rails terminated in another cavern but this one was quite a bit smaller than the one they had just left. Some empty trolley cages lay abandoned, beside the track. They peered around but there was no sign of anyone. Directly above their heads was a vertical shaft and as they looked, they could see a small square of grey light way above them. Two thick nylon ropes hung down from the shaft, one of which was attached to a small platform made out of wood. A metal handrail was fixed to this on three sides with a hinged bar making up the fourth side. Ropes had been attached to all four corners on the platform and were secured to a large metal ring some ten feet above from which one of the thick ropes was also tied. Terry grasped the loose rope which was threaded through a pulley fixed to the side of the platform and gently pulled it. As soon as he did this, the platform lifted off the floor. He let the rope slowly slide through his fingers again and the platform returned to the ground.

"This must be the bottom of the old pump house shaft and this is how our friends have exited the tunnels with the flasks. There must be some sort of pulley arrangement or counter weight system to allow this platform to be lifted up and down as easily as this with people or goods on it. Looking at it, I think it can quite easily be raised or lowered just by feeding this loose rope through this wheel fixed to the side and either pulled it through or letting it go depending whether or not you want to go up or down. Our decision is, do we go up and hope nobody is still there because if there is, we are going to be sitting ducks, stuck halfway up with nowhere to hide? Or do we back track and try to get out another way?"

"I think we will have to chance it, Boss. If we back track, we will lose them for sure with no guarantee we would even be able to find our way out in time."

"You are right, of course. Let's go. You see anything move up that shaft, you let rip, do you hear?"

"You got it, Boss."

They stepped onto the platform and Terry started to gently pull on the rope. It jerked slightly and then they were off. It rose into the air quite steadily as Terry hauled on it but much more smoothly and soundless than either of them had expected.

Nothing above them moved and they strained their ears to hear the slightest sound. The platform swayed alarmingly, occasionally grating against the rough rock sides of the shaft. They were rapidly approaching the top, so Terry slowed down pulling the rope through the wheel. They crouched down as very gently the platforms handrail breached the opening. Davy straightened his legs and peered over the lip of the shaft, his gun hand extended ready to take a shot if necessary. He made an upward movement with his spare hand, so Terry hauled on the rope again until the bottom of the platform was level with the top lip of the shaft. He tied the rope off to prevent it slipping. Rain splashed down, soaking them. They looked around but nothing moved. They stepped off onto the concrete plinth surrounding the shaft. A large and heavy tripod surrounded it with a complex pulley arrangement fixed to the top. Two very heavy metal covers lay to one side.

"I know where we are, Davy," said Terry. "This is the old mine pump house at the edge of the cliffs, just below the wood near the footpath which runs back to the house. Jason and I stood just over there looking at a ledge on the point over there where he thought he had seen something."

"Had he?"

"Well, in retrospect, I think he did and it was possibly our big furry friend. But it was all too vague. The weather was about the same as it is tonight, awful!

"Anyway, this place appears to be deserted. I wonder where they have all gone?"

They must have had at least a truck or a large van to get this rig put up here, mused Davy. "Let's have a look around."

The rain swept around them in sheets blown by a strong gale force wind coming straight off the Atlantic making visibility poor. They could hear the surf smashing into the rocks below and at times foam from it was blasted high into the air giving the appearance of large flakes of snow.

The area around the old mine was carefully searched but they found nothing. Terry walked over to the track leading away from the mine and bent down to inspect the tyre tread marks which were clearly defined in the mud.

"Hmmm! Two vehicles, I think, Davy. The problem we have is where will they have gone and how we could follow them even if we knew where that was?"

Brent said the flasks would be out of the country by tomorrow, didn't he? mused Davy.

"How would you do that? Boat? No! There no suitable harbour to load them near here. Also, I think, very unlikely to be by road. To easy to be stopped, especially at the port of departure. The only other option would be by air. Yes, that's got to be it! That would be the most logical," Davy theorised out loud.

"I agree, Davy, but where could you load a small aircraft locally without drawing attention to yourself? You know the area far better than I do, so where do you suggest?"

Davy thought for a moment or two.

"Well," he said slowly. "There are two possible airfields within easy reach and out of these only one would be suitable because it would not be monitored by the authorities. It's a private one. It used to be a fighter drome during the Second World War and is now used by a gliding club and private aircraft. This time of the year and in this weather, I doubt if there would be anyone there. Yes, Boss, it has gotta be. Bowden Airfield! But it is nearly five miles away from here." Davy speculated.

"Right! I bow to your expert advice, my boy. We will double back to Trelease House and pick up my car. I take it you know how to get there?"

"No probs. Used to go up there to trap rabbits and do a bit of courting, many years ago when my dad lived near here."

"Great! Let's go."

They set off up the track leading back to the house at a steady run. Davy's bag was slung over his shoulder and his arm was wrapped around it as if it was the only possession he had ever had. The rain continued to slash down in torrents making visibility poor and the track slippery. Their feet slithered in the mud even with the heavy cleated soles on their boots and water dripped down their necks as they doubled along almost at a full run and they made good time along the track and shortly, they were rewarded with the gleam of lights from Trelease House. Terry was panting hard as he jumped up the steps to the front door which he banged on heavily.

He was just about to hit the door again when it cracked open a few inches and a nozzle of a gun appeared in the space.

"Identify yourself," a voice rasped.

"Major Terry Knight and Captain Davy Bates," Terry gasped, trying to suck in enough air to speak.

A torch was shone into his face and then the door was swung open wide at that and the remaining guard that had been left by Dr Faulkner stood looking at them open mouthed. Suddenly, remembering himself, he stood back and saluted.

"I didn't expect to see you coming from this direction, sir."

"Not enough time to explain, soldier. I just need the keys to my car." Terry snapped. "My wife and son, they are OK?"

"Yes, sir," the guard replied.

Just then, Lydia charged down the stairs in her dressing gown closely followed by Jason.

"I heard voices," she whispered as she flung herself into Terry's arms. "Natasha?"

"Not yet, my darling. In good time, I promise. We are in hot pursuit of the bad guys who may know about Natasha. I am not sure." Terry panted, gently unwinding Lydia's arm from around his neck. "Jason, please, look after your mum." as he could see the tears forming in Lydia's eyes.

"Sure thing, Dad."

Terry rushed over to a hook on the wall and snatched his car keys off it, gave Lydia a huge hug and kissed her on the cheek.

"Tell Dr Faulkner we think they are about to fly the flasks out via Bowden Airfield. If he is able to offer us any assistance, we will greatly appreciate the help," Terry ordered to the guard.

"Yes, sir. I will put a message out on the short wave radio immediately. Kyle, sir? Is he OK?" said the guard, obviously concerned with his friend and colleague.

Terry glanced over to him and his face softened.

"I am sorry, man. He didn't make it." Terry paused. "Sorry but we have to go."

Terry and Davy turned and ran back out of the house. Terry clicked the key fob to unlock the car. They jumped in and Terry gunned the engine, fastening their safety belts as he did so. He swung the powerful four by four around and, with tyres spinning, spurting gravel, he roared up the drive.

Dawn was just beginning to show in the eastern sky, the edges of the dark, scudding clouds flecked with an edge of pink as the sun was slowly rising, but still slightly below the horizon. The rain had eased slightly as had the wind, showing a promise of a better day's weather.

Terry was hunched over the steering wheel, obviously still in pain, concentrating on keeping the heavy car on the narrow lanes which criss-crossed the country in this area while following Davy's instructions. Luckily, there was no other traffic to contend with. At the speed they had been travelling, that would have made things interesting, bearing in mind how narrow the lanes were. Sweat trickled down his face, leaving streaks through the dirt, mud and dust caked to his skin. Davy appeared to be in a similar condition except, of course, he was not injured. He was also 15 years younger than Terry and that makes a big difference to someone's endurance. Looking at

Terry, Davy realised that he was nearing the end of what a man could endure. The grim, determined set of his chin, his face with his bloodshot eyes all scrunched up, highlighting the lines etched into the face. He could feel it himself. He ached in every muscle and he looked at his reflection in the sun visor mirror and barely recognised the person he saw there.

"Nearly there now, Boss," he said quietly. "Just turn left in 200 yards and the entrance will be on the right. We need to park up near here just in case they have put a guard at the entrance. If they have, this will prove we have the right place."

Terry grunted and swung the Volvo off the road and through into an open field gateway and turned it behind the high hedge, stopped and switched off the engine. They sat there for a few seconds but nothing moved. Terry swung his door open and with another grunt, this time in pain, slid out of the driving seat and closed the door quietly. He put his hand against his chest and massaged it.

"Are you OK, Boss?" Davy inquired, concerned for him.

Terry grimaced and nodded.

"You look like shit, Davy!"

"Have you looked at yourself?"

A painful smile slowly spread across Terry's face.

"I'm keeping myself in suspense and anticipation of that wonderful surprise when I do. I might need a bit Lydia's make-up before I do, I think."

Davy grinned. "Well, you haven't lost your sense of humour, have you?"

Terry gave him a really dark look.

"Right then! We will keep in the shadow of this hedge and see if we can get up to the entrance without anyone seeing us, just in case there are guards there. If there are, we will have to deal with them before we can get closer to those hangers over there," he said pointing to the large buildings nearby.

"Er, Deal with them? Like, er, terminate?"

"I am in no mood to play patsy pudding with anyone who now gets in our way." Terry grated.

Davy nodded and then rummaged in his bag, fishing out two sets of camouflage netting, one of which he handed to Terry and he pulled his over his head, adjusting as he did so. He then helped Terry with his as he was struggling to fit it properly because of his damaged ribs. Every arm movement was becoming more difficult as his muscles were beginning to cramp up and sending spasms of pain across his body.

They crouched down as they followed the edge of the hedge to where it joined a second hedge which ran alongside the roadway to the entrance.

"Stay there, Boss, while I go to check on the entrance."

Davy slipped away like ghost in the half light. A few moments later, he returned, holding up two fingers.

"We guessed right, Boss. Heavily armed as well," he whispered. "There is a small opening in the hedge almost opposite where they are. We can get close up and personal if we are careful how we go."

"Let's do it," Terry whispered back.

Very carefully and quietly they sidled up alongside the hedge, crawling the last few yards until the gap became close. Terry peered through the grass at the entrance. A small building was alongside it and one of the guards was lounging against the doorway, an AK47 automatic hung on a strap across his chest. The second guard was nowhere to be seen.

Suddenly, a voice called from inside the hut and the guard outside turned to face the doorway and said something. Terry didn't hesitate. In a second, he had leapt to his feet and crossed the intervening space. He had almost reached the man when perhaps some sixth sense warned the guard and he started to turn towards Terry. Too late! Terry grabbed him in a neck lock, pulling him over backwards while his arms tightened around the man neck stifling any cry of alarm. There was a click and the man went limp in Terry's arms with a broken neck. Terry slowly let him down onto the ground but even though the guard had been unable to make a sound, the scuffling had alerted the other man in the hut. He came barrelling out of the doorway and his eyes widened at seeing Terry. He swung his AK47 desperately towards him but Terry was there ahead of him. A commando knife had suddenly appeared in Terry's hand which was flicked expertly in a silver flash burying itself in the man's throat. His feet skidded out from under him and he went over backwards, gurgling. The heels of his feet jerked and thrashed a few times on the ground and then were still.

Terry bent down and retrieved his knife, sliding it into a sheath on his belt. The whole episode had taken seconds. Davy joined Terry and helped him drag the two bodies into the hut.

"Bloody Hell! You haven't lost your touch, have you?" Davy muttered admiringly as they closed the door.

They left the entrance road and crawled towards the hangers. A large truck was parked close to the hanger's doors, bright lights illuminating the interior and they could see some figures moving around inside in front of a twin engine light aircraft. A Land Rover and a car could also be seen alongside it.

“Bingo,” said Terry with satisfaction. “Looks like we are just in time to as if I am not mistaken, they look as though the loading has been done and they are getting ready to leave.”

“How are we going to handle this, Boss? We are seriously outnumbered!”

“You must be getting old, Davy,” said Terry with a self-satisfied grin. “You never used to worry about the odds. We have surprise on our side which should help. Have you still got any of those whizz bangs you were using earlier? If you have, then that would be a good start. Rough ’em up a bit. Whatever happens, we have to stop that plane from taking off.”

Davy nodded.

“Leave it to me. I’ll sidle down around the back and loose off my Davy special. You can then come in from the other side in the confusion and we can catch them in a cross fire. They won’t know what hit them.” Davy gave a little chuckle.

“Sounds good to me.” Terry agreed.

Davy slid away in the gloom and within seconds had disappeared from view. Terry carefully and slowly crept ever closer to the hanger entrance until he could hear the mutter of foreign voices. He checked his gun and automatic pistol and lay down in the grass to wait. From his position, he could see most of the inside of the hanger. He had the ear piece of his radio comms fixed firmly into his ear which Davy had supplied from his goody bag.

Suddenly, his receiver clicked twice, paused and then clicked again twice. This was Davy, sending him a prearranged message meaning, “I am in position and are you ready?”

Terry doubled click back. The ‘I am ready’ signal.

A few seconds clicked past. Then a whoosh and an explosion as the projectile hit the lorry. It was instantly swathed in flames. A man screamed as he leapt out of the drivers cab with his arms alight and ran to get clear. Too late! The truck exploded in a kaleidoscope of colours, bits of it flying high into the air and showering down in a lethal hail of red hot metal some of which hit two other men which violently terminated their lives.

Chaos ensued. Men were running in all direction, some waving their guns, others screaming in pain, shouting in foreign voices. A couple of them were wielding fire extinguishers, trying to control the flames but with little effect. The magnesium in Davy's projectile was burning through just about everything. Just then another whooshing sound and one of the cars disappeared in a blaze of flame and within a few seconds exploded spectacularly as its petrol tank caught fire. There was a number of 50 gallon drums close by and these started to catch fire adding to the mayhem, some taking off and hurtling fifty feet into the air before exploding in a massive fireball, again showering the surrounding area with even more shrapnel.

Terry, leap to his feet and crossed the intervening grass at the full run, unseen by the people in the hanger who were silhouetted against the flames and desperately trying to escape the inferno. More barrels exploded. They must have contained aviation fuel by the way they caught fire so easily. A man ran towards him with his jacket on fire, saw Terry at the last minute and tried to swing his gun to bear. Far to slow! Terry swung his arm and his automatic spat death. The man skidded onto his back still burning.

Another guard charged towards him, firing wildly. Terry snapped off two shots which both hit home. The man stumbled forward and collapsed nearly at Terry's feet.

Firing was now coming from the rear of the hanger where Davy was obviously in contact with the enemy. Suddenly this stopped. Other guards were now firing at Terry from behind steel pillars as he took dived for cover.

A voice shouted out something and the firing ceased. The flames continued to crackle, casting big shadows and billowing thick black smoke.

"Major Terry. If that is you out there, please, do not shoot as I have something for you. Please, look carefully," a voice shouted.

"I am coming out where you can see me," it added.

Terry peered through the gloomy smoked filled hanger and spotted movement near the small office building within the hanger. He started with shock.

Slowly moving towards him was Ho flanked by two heavily armed men. It was not that that made Terry react violently but the person Ho was pushing in front of him while holding a gun to their head.

"Oh my God," Terry whispered to himself. "Natasha!"

"You fire, she dies," Ho shouted.

"Kill him, Dad," Natasha screamed.

"Please, do nothing foolish, Major. I will kill her and then you. Put your gun down. NOW!"

Terry slowly stood up and lowered his gun.

"That's better, Major." And then Ho gave a loud laugh.

"Almost, but not quite. You really are persistent, aren't you?"

Terry looked at Natasha's dirty streaked face. She was exhausted. That was plain to see. Her bandage was still wound around her head but a dribble of blood was slowly seeping down the side of her forehead from it. His mind was spinning. How was this possible? Where had she been? How did she become their prisoner? What could he do to save her and himself? Where was Davy?

All these thoughts cascaded through his brain. His thought process was interrupted by Ho.

"You are just a little too late, my friend. We are leaving in a minute or two. Your little girl here was SO pleased to see us. She practically begged us to take her away, so we did. I thought she might come in handy and so it has happened." Ho laughed again, an unpleasant sound as it was not a laugh born from humour.

"Where is my friend Davy?" Terry asked.

"Oh! I think you may find him back there with one or two bullets in him." He returned jerking a thumb over his shoulder. "Don't worry. Much as I would like to put a bullet in your head, you may not believe me when I say that I do not make war on women especially pretty ones like your daughter. We will just leave you here when we fly off. Yes, Major. We are all loaded with the flasks so I have no further use for being here any longer. Ha! Ha!"

"No regrets for Kevin then?" Terry spat out.

"Kevin? Regrettable! He had served his purpose but then one less person to share the money with. Both he and Trelease had fantastic brains and their research was nothing short of amazing."

Ho cocked his head to one side, listening intently.

"I think some of your friends are coming so I will be on my way!" He exclaimed.

A faint hum could be heard, rapidly becoming louder with by the second. Helicopters!

Ho turned to the men that bordered him. "Take them away and tie them up, securely!"

Natasha and her father were dragged into the office and tied to chairs. Terry looked out the window and saw Ho and some of his men climb up the steps into the plane whose engine now fired up and slowly ran up to full power. Ho came to the door and was about to close it when to Terry's amazement, he saw Davy crawling painfully towards the steps. Ho spotted him and jumped back out of the plane drawing his gun as he did so. He raised him arm and levelled his gun at Davy. At that moment, several things happened all at once. Terry saw Davy bring his arm back and something flew past Ho into the aircrafts cabin.

"Noooo," Terry screamed and Ho, not seeming to notice, pumped two bullets into Davy who jerked violently. The aircraft was starting to move out of the hanger and Ho turned and had to run after it. He grabbed the steps and pulled himself up and into the cabin. The steps were collapsed and folded up into the body of the aircraft. Ho took one last look around and then slammed the door shut. The aircrafts engine whined into a higher pitch and slowly made its way onto the apron where it revved even higher and it increased speed and disappeared out onto the tarmac where it quickly accelerated to the end of the runway before turning and without stopping, roared down it to lift off into the lightening sky and out over the cliffs towards the sea. Only its navigation lights showed where it was in the night sky. The remaining men leapt into the Range Rover, the only remaining vehicle and sped off.

Terry leapt to his feet and rammed the legs of the chair into the gap between the wall and the radiator and wrenched himself backwards. There was a splintering sound as the legs broke of and forcing the radiator partially off the wall. The ropes holding Terry immediately slackened and he was able, with some difficulty, to untie himself. He turned to Natasha and after untying her, wrapped his arms around her and hugged her as hard as he could. Tears cascaded down both their faces as they hung together.

"Explanations will come later! I must look after Davy," Terry murmured into her ear and gently disengaged from her arms.

Terry ran out of the office and across the hanger to where Davy lay.

He bent down and cradled Davy's head. Tears formed in his eyes as he saw what the bullets had done to his friend. Blood was oozing from numerous wounds. Natasha joined him and put a hand out to grip her father's shoulder as he knelt beside Davy.

"No, no, no," he kept on saying over and over again. "They have got away with it. After everything we have been through!"

"Not on your fucking life, Boss!" Davy twitched in Terry's arm. "Watch the sky, Boss, watch the sky," Davy whispered.

"Natasha. Go back to the office and see if you can find a phone. There should be one in there, hopefully working and ring for an ambulance. Urgent!" Terry ordered.

Davy grimaced with pain and a trickle of blood ran out of his mouth. He coughed and more gushed out, this time in a steady stream.

"Don't bother, Boss, too late," he croaked.

Natasha hesitated, took one look at her father and ran back across the hanger towards the office.

Suddenly, with an ear splitting howl, two black helicopters flashed past overhead, one flaring abruptly, to hover briefly in front of the hanger, before setting down. The wheels had not even touched the ground before a group of men had leapt out and fanned out across the apron in front of the hanger. All were heavily armed and dressed completely in black with ski masks drawn up tightly against their faces. The helicopter's engines roared again as it lifted off and was replaced with the second one. This did exactly the same as the first, disgorging another band of men who split into two groups, who doubled off out of sight, one to the right and one to the left with the obvious intention of surrounding the hanger complex.

This second one lifted off again like its predecessor and disappeared. Terry could see the navigation lights of Ho's aircraft becoming higher in the sky when the sky suddenly light up with a gigantic mushroom of fire. A few seconds later, the sound of the massive explosion rumbled across the airfield, rattling the windows and doors. Glowing bits of the aircraft sparkled briefly in the sky before rapidly falling down and down to disappear out of sight somewhere over the sea beyond the cliffs.

Terry looked down at Davy. A little smile creased the corners of Davy's lips.

"Did it work?" he whispered. "I wish I could have seen it but it is getting so dark in here."

Terry held his arms around Davy's shoulders, tears starting to trickle down his own face streaking the dirt caked on it.

"Another of your Davy specials, I suppose," he said.

Davy twitched again and more blood bubbled out of his mouth.

"Naw! Just the timer and explosive charge I kept from the cellar."

Terry was aware that Natasha had returned and was standing behind him.

"The ambulance is on its way," she said in a low voice.

Davy was struggling to breathe and was fading fast only too obviously.

"It…was…a…priv-il-ege to have one…last…jolly, Boss."

With that, his head rolled slightly to one side and another flood of blood poured from his mouth and then he was still.

Terry laid Davy's head very gently to the ground and pulling off his jacket, covered Davy with it.

Armed men surrounded them, standing quietly in a semi-circle. A figure pushed through the ring and approached Terry. A hand gripped his arm and the ski mask was pushed up to reveal Dr Faulkner. He was breathing heavily from exertion. "God damn! I am getting too old for all this charging around in and out of aircraft and vehicles, always in a rush. I am never able to do it in a relaxed way." He looked down at the covered body and sighed.

"Damn! I am so sorry, Major. We came as quickly as we could but just a few minutes too late it appears. What was the explosion? Was that Davy's doing?"

"It's over, Doctor. That was the aircraft that contained all the flasks and a guy called Ho who was in cahoots with Kevin and Harvey and is." Terry corrected himself. "Was, I think, the link with Korea."

"Well, that is at least some good news." The Doctor looked around.

"Jesus Christ, Major! Did you and Davy start World War three in here or what?" he said, looking around at all the devastation in the hanger.

The wreckage from the truck and the car were still smoking, black oily tendrils of the smoke filling the roof with chunks of the vehicles spread all over the hanger. Still burning oil drums littered the area with a flotsam of other rubbish strewn everywhere. Several bodies lay in grotesque shapes in the flickering light.

Terry wearily stood up, now more composed and looked at him.

"There are a few of his soldiers still around. They left just as you arrived in a Range Rover."

Just then, one of the men accompanying the Doctor approached him, still talking into his comms mike.

"We have them all, sir. They didn't want to come quietly so our guys had to take them out after a short fire fight. They are all dead."

"Tell them a well done from me," the Doctor replied. "Will you clear up here while I debrief the Major? There is to be nothing to be left, clean sweep. OK?" he ordered.

"Very well, sir. It will be done." The man saluted and with some of his platoon following, ran back out.

"I think we ought to get you and your daughter back to your house where we can talk in more comfort, if that is all right with you?" the Doctor asked.

Terry nodded. "Fine, sir, just fine. I have a few questions to ask my daughter as well." He looked at Natasha and for the first time for quite a while gave a small smile. He slid an arm around her waist and together with the Doctor walked to the hanger entrance where one of the black helicopters was putting down on the apron outside.

"We may as well go back in style. It will also be an awful lot quicker," said the Doctor.

"What about my car?" Terry asked.

"Don't worry, I'll get that returned to your house shortly."

They climbed into the helicopter and were joined by two of the armed guards. The engines screamed and then they were airborne and heading out across the countryside.

* * * * *

Chapter Nineteen
Explanations

The look on Lydia and Jason's face said it all. Sophia had come over to the house earlier in the evening to help comfort them. They had, at first, been alarmed as the helicopter first made a circle of the house before gently setting down in the driveway.

Terry and Natasha were enveloped in tight bear hugs as they vacated the helicopter with the Doctor following, together with his two bodyguards as they made their way up the steps into the house.

"Easy, babe!" Terry exclaimed. "I'm still very sore."

Lydia ignored his protestations and just hugged him tighter.

"I'll put the kettle on while you and Natasha get cleaned up. You both look exhausted," she said.

The Doctor smiled. "You do as your missus tells you Major and come back down when you are ready and then we can have a chat as to what you found out and what you did. OK?"

Jason helped his father and sister up the stairs and into their respective bathrooms and returned back down to help his mother who was now busy in the kitchen preparing bacon and cheese sandwiches and of course the essential mugs of tea for all the hungry and thirsty men.

The sun was now well up and had the promise of a fine day ahead after the recent storms.

Eventually, after quite a long wait, Terry and Natasha returned back downstairs and they all gathered in the large lounge to await the various reports of what had transpired.

Terry looked across at Natasha. "I think you should tell us, first of all, what happened to you after you locked yourself in the hidden tunnel behind your fireplace."

Natasha nodded and recounted her tale of how she found herself unable to get back into her bedroom and had stumbled through the dark passages until she had tripped and knocked herself out, only to regain consciousness in the hidden cavern with her saviour. Then on to her horror when she realised what this creature was and what he had told her about how he had been incarcerated and was hidden in the mine shafts and that he intended to hold her a captive indefinitely.

"You should have seen this thing. He was monstrous. I never saw Father and from what I saw of the younger one, I think I am glad I didn't." He spoke a sort of broken English which his mother had taught him. She was buried in one of the caverns having died in a gas attack. He told me the retribution his father meted out to the men that did it. Although, I have to say, he was very gentle with me and treated me with extreme kindness. He appeared to be under the illusion that he was in love with me. He made me sleep on a rock ledge covered in furs which, funnily enough, was very comfortable and after the clout on my head, I was very glad to lie down.

“I must have slept for some time because the first thing I remember when I woke up was a whole lot of guns going off in the distance. I could hear this creature pacing up and down, snorting and moaning and then it suddenly took off down one of the tunnels. I felt that this was my chance to escape, possibly my only one, so I ran away down a tunnel in the opposite direction. I seemed to be going for miles until I heard more shooting but this time much closer. Then I heard a loud bang and saw a flash in the distance. The light from the flash went on for a while and enabled me to speed up as I could see better.”

Terry interrupted her. “That must have been Davy’s special which he fired at the goons when they tried to ambush us when we had them on the run.”

Terry interrupted her again. “Hang on a minute. This happened after we had killed it in the main cavern? You said Father?”

Terry started with shock and stared at her. “Are you telling me that there were TWO of those beasts down in the tunnels? Oh…My…God!”

“Yes, Dad! Father and Son. Anyway,” said Natasha, continuing, “I suddenly heard sounds behind me and realised the creature was catching up with me. I ran towards where the sounds and the flash had come from and rushed straight out of the tunnel I was in into another larger one and right into this bunch of armed men. They grabbed me tied my hands together and half dragged me along with them. All of a sudden, there was total chaos as this creature charged out of a side tunnel and tried to grab me back. The men I was with tried to fight it off but it got hold of one of them and literally tore him to pieces in front of me. Dad, it was awful! The poor man screamed and screamed but it didn't do any good. It shook him like a dog with a rat. The other men, when they realised their mate was obviously dead, started to shoot at it. I think they hit it a few times because it howled and roared and then disappeared back into the tunnel it had come from."

Terry nodded grimly. "If it was anything like its father, then it takes a lot of killing. This explains an awful lot. I will tell my story in a minute."

Natasha carried on. "They then dragged me to some kind of hoist and then into the back of a lorry packed with a lot of funny kind of bottles. I then arrived at the airfield and the rest you know."

Terry took over and recounted what had happened to the three of them from the time they had entered the tunnel from Natasha's bedroom. The horrific events in the main storage cavern where Kyle had been shot dead by Kevin Brent and their difficulty and reluctance to kill the Gargoyle as they now called the creature. He described how he and Davy had followed the tunnels in hot pursuit, hoping to prevent the flasks being removed. The way Davy had fired his special homemade weapon which succeeded in preventing them from being ambushed.

Terry told them about how they had heard the awful moaning in the distance and then the shooting which they could not understand which went on when they were not the target which now became clear as to how and why this had happened.

"Now I know how it was when I was attempting to escape from the tunnels myself and something seized my ankle and I managed to break free and then found myself in the middle of the marsh, I could not understand how it tracked me down so quickly. It is now obvious as there were TWO of them. What a total nightmare!

"Davy and I carried on following the bad guys but by the time we were able to get out of the tunnels, they were gone."

Terry went on to describe how they returned to the house to get his car, how Davy narrowed down where they might have gone to escape with the flasks and their continued pursuit, to the killing of the two guards at the entrance gate to the airfield which had confirmed that they had the right venue at Bowden. The way Davy attacked from the rear of the hanger while Terry entered from the front.

Terry was obviously delighted and amazed, even in the circumstances, at finding Natasha there alive and well.

How Davy had, even with his dying breathes, had managed to foil Ho and destroy the aircraft containing the flasks with Ho still inside with his cronies.

Terry gave a deep sigh. "I can't believe he is gone. We had been through so much. If it wasn't for him, we would not have survived our kidnapping in the dungeons and we would have let Ho get away with the flasks. And that is only part of it. All the times he saved the lives of his platoon and not to mention me, which happened far too often."

There was a long silence in the room with them all of them with their own thoughts.

After a while, the Doctor gave a polite cough and in a slightly gruff voice said, "We will all miss Davy and the likes of Kyle and all the others who have given their lives in the constant fight to keep this great country and our citizens safe. Be in no doubt that we owe them a huge debt of gratitude which we will never be able to pay. We will NEVER forget them."

The Doctor continued,

"I have great belief in a statement by the great Edmund Burke which goes something like this: For evil men to succeed all it needs is for good men to stand by and do nothing.

"I am not too sure I have repeated it exactly as he said it but I think, close enough for us to identify the meaning behind his words. I try to work to carry out the sentiment of these words for which I have a tremendous regard for and believe in them for the greater good of the many.

"As we sit here, my men will be carrying out my orders to clear up the airfield and surrounding area to the extent that we will be able to issue a statement to any interested parties that the disruption was due to a drug raid in this area and as a result a light aircraft took off from the airfield and due to severe engine failure, crashed into the sea with no survivors.

"Obviously, there will be people living nearby who will have heard the explosions and will be wondering what had gone on. The police have now already created a no go perimeter outside of ours so we should be able to complete our clean up without interruption.

"As you know we were alerted to your situation and came just as soon as we could put together a suitable team. It is with extreme regret we could not get here sooner.

"Having heard from you all about the situation which existed underground, we will send our teams down to the caverns to clear them out. Additionally, I think we need to recover both Kyle's body together with the other ones, taking the Gargoyle's body away for further testing and remove Miss Wendy Winston's remains so that she may be given a proper funeral which I am sure is what her mother will want. I do not think it would be helpful to tell her of the full horror of what transpired and it might cause an unnecessary breach of security. I think the best way of an explanation will be to inform her that her remains were found during a search of the caverns and that our conclusion is that she must have fallen down a shaft all those years ago.

“We will then seal up the caverns at both ends to prevent them ever being used again and also as a safety measure to ensure that nothing nasty could escape just in case we missed anything.

“Since we last met, Hal has progressed with the investigation into the items recovered from the cellars and I have received his preliminarily report. It is clear that a serum WAS produced by Harvey Trelease and Kevin Brent that gave the results we have witnessed in the Gargoyle who apparently was unaffected by either gas or biological agents but with disastrous and horrific results on this poor creature’s body.

“They did not appear to have been able to remove the dioxins from the original product, namely, Agent Orange. It maybe they were not unduly concerned with doing this and were concentrating more on the process of forming this invincible monster. Whatever the aim was, it is has been contained and we must thank God for that. Hal considers that it will be impossible to duplicate the serum without an actual sample of it. As we know, this has been completely destroyed when the aircraft blew up.”

The Doctor looked around at the assembled faces and continued again.

“You will all be bound by the Official Secrets Act. Ladies and Gentlemen, this never happened and if any questions are asked, all knowledge of any of this will be completely denied.

I hope this is implicitly understood." He smiled at them. "I would like to thank you all for the part you have all played in preventing an unbelievable escalation of the secret warfare which we are engaged in at this present time. You have been amazing!"

They all nodded in agreement.

Doctor Faulkner, then took his leave, shaking hands with everybody before boarding the helicopter with his guards. The man who had been looking after Lydia and Jason left with the last vehicle belonging to Group.

Terry gazed around at his family. "I think we should all have a good hot shower or bath and then have something to eat before catching up with some sleep and try and get our lives back on track. I don't know about you guys but I am completely bushed."

* * * * *

Epilogue

As Doctor Falkner had stated, Wendy Winston's remains were removed and her funeral was held locally. Mrs Minnie Winston was now able to grieve properly for her long dead daughter and the service was attended by many people from the town which naturally included the Knight Family.

Davy was buried in the local cemetery with full military honours. Some people commented on the large number of sombre but tough looking individuals who attended but no explanation was forthcoming.

A new General Practitioner arrived to take over the surgery recently vacated by Dr Jackson. He was a young guy and went to work with dedication and an obvious passion for his work.

Terry had been very withdrawn since the death of Davy and spent long periods of time walking the cliff path alone and sometimes Lydia found him sitting on a rock gazing out to sea. On this occasion, Lydia went to look for him and found him sitting on his favourite rock and sat down beside him. She slid a comforting arm round his broad shoulders.

"I know you are missing Davy, my darling, but what else is wrong? I know something is. Tell me," she commanded.

For a while, Terry just sat there still gazing at the sea and then replied, speaking very quietly.

"There is still an unanswered question which has been going around and around in my head and I think I have now just about worked it out. I need to go into town and sort it out."

Lydia tightened her arm around him. "If that is what you need to do, then do it. I am with you whatever you decide."

Terry turned and gazed into her eyes. "I love you, babe and always will. No man could ask more from a woman for the support you give me and the unconditional love you give me.

"I do not want to do what I think I must but I have just one more thing to do. Then I think Davy will be able to sleep the big sleep a little more easily."

With that, they got to their feet and arm in arm, slowly walked back to Trelease House. Terry drew Lydia close and kissed her. Then he turned and climbed into his car and roared off up the drive.

A short while later, he parked the car and walked a short distance along the street until he came to a familiar doorway. He opened the door and walked through to the reception which was empty. Without hesitation, he went to a door behind the reception desk and pushed it open.

Mr John Desmond Hargreaves was slumped in his chair holding a glass of red wine. The nearly empty bottle was at the side of his desk. The whole office was a mess of paper files and documents. He jumped visibly at the sight of Terry.

"Mr Knight! You made me jump. Do we have an appointment?" he slurred

Terry stood still and silent in front of him for a moment.

"No, I don't but you do, one with your conscience, that's if you have one," Terry said grimly.

Hargreaves eyes flickered and his face paled.

"I have no idea what you are talking about and if you think you can come barging into my office making threats and being belligerent, then think again!"

"You are really something, aren't you? You nearly got away with it, didn't you? But, you see, I got to thinking. It was all about the money, wasn't it? Where did the funding for the work at Trelease House come from? Who paid and how did the money come into the country? Who paid for the hired thugs and again, how? I suppose it was quite easy to work out a scheme to wash all the money through property deals which or may not have been genuine and then slide some away to pay the bills?

"You told me Trelease had already died before you came here and you did not know who owned the house after him as you had never met him and didn't know him. It was all lies, wasn't it?

"You were the money man, weren't you? It was you who let the cat out of the bag by telling your now dead friends what my background was and maybe even linking in Davy. It would not have taken much research to find out that we both had military backgrounds together and put two and two together. I could not work out to start with, just how our Asian thugs got to know so quickly. I will bet your friends were not too impressed with you selling the house to someone like me, were they? They then had to move quickly to try and sort things out. But they didn't reckon on the Gargoyle messing everything up.

"No wonder you are so nervous. The people who financed this deal must, by now, be wondering what went wrong and it will be only a question of time before they come knocking on your door wanting their money back. Am I right?"

Hargreaves face had turned ashen. "They will kill me, I know this. You must help me. I have money. Lots of it. It is all yours if you help me. Please."

Hargreaves reached over and opened a drawer and withdrew a large package. He threw it down onto the desk. "200,000 pounds and it is all yours if you help me disappear."

Terry looked at him with undisguised disgust.

"I will take the money but not to help you. Davy's girlfriend is penniless and about to be thrown out of the pub. She is also expecting Davy's baby. This should enable her to pay for the pub and maybe a bit to pay for the things she will need for the child. I will do something to help you though."

"Anything you say, I will do," said Hargreaves, his face bathed in sweat.

Terry picked up the package and stuffed it into a bag he had over his shoulder and walked towards the door.

"Wait. What about me? You said you would help." Hargreaves blustered.

"Oh, yes, I did, didn't I?"

Terry slid a hand into his bag and pulled something out. He turned to face Hargreaves.

"Try this for size. But please, do me and everyone else a favour, will you? And do it right."

A small automatic pistol banged onto the desk.

"It has only one bullet in it and the safety catch is off. If this is not an option, then when I come back, I will do it for you." Terry grated.

He turned on his heel and walked out into the street and nearly collided with Sophia coming the other way. He took her by the arm and gently guided her away.

"John, can't see you for a while?" he said softly.

At that moment, there was a muffled bang from behind them.

Terry pulled out his mobile and dialled 999. "Police, please."

A brief pause and then, "I think I need to report a suicide. Yes, that's correct. Just now. Mr Hargreaves, the Estate Agent. In his office. My name is Major Terry Knight. Thank you. I will wait for you."

Sophia stared at Terry wordlessly.

"Go to Jason, please, Sophia. This was for the best. He was in it right up to his miserable neck."

Sophia's eyes filled with tears and nodded, turned and ran back to where her car was parked and drove off.

Days later, Terry went to see Di, Davy's girlfriend and gave her the money in the package. At first she would not take it and it took all of Terry's powers of persuasion to get her to accept it. He told her it was compensation issued to Davy posthumously from the special forces and it was her duty as next of kin to accept it. Also because of the nature of the work involved, normal routes could not be taken. Terry considered that the slight white lie was acceptable considering the circumstances.

It took quite a while for things to settle down but it appeared that someone in authority had had a quiet word in the police's ears. Terry was quite certain who that someone was but no names were ever mentioned.

Jason went back to work at the surf shop and moved out of Trelease House and together with Sophia, went and moved into a lovely two bed roomed cottage close to Minnie's coffee shop. They went over to see Terry and Lydia at the weekend and after a superb lunch told them their news; Sophia was now three months pregnant! The whole family were delighted, none more so than Natasha, who danced around them excitedly exclaiming that she had never been an Auntie before.

There was quite a bit of excitement in the town one day when a body was found washed up on the nearby beach, very badly decomposed.

The police were called and roped off the area. A short while later some men turned up and to the surprise of the watching locals, removed the remains of the body while wearing biological suits and it was then taken away in a large refrigerated van. The man who had stumbled across it, told anyone who wanted to listen that he thought it must have been an alien from outer space as he had never seen anything so gross in his entire life.

"Fangs like a lion and huge claws with lumps of hair all over the body. It was so huge it couldn't have been human."

The Knight family listened to the tales and reckoned they knew better.

"I think it was badly wounded and managed to live for a short while. Maybe it fell over the cliff or maybe it jumped. We will never know." Terry surmised.

Natasha resumed her studies at university, having completely recovered from her ordeal.

Terry and Lydia continue to live at Trelease House and the landline is now connected. The mobile signal is now in place but at times hard to get.

Tranquillity has now returned to the cliffs and valleys around the big house.

However, some locals still talk about the marsh and the surrounding area in whispers. Some say they have still heard moaning sounds drifting across the valley on very dark nights.

But that is not possible, is it? It must be the wind!!!

THE END